PITIFUL CRIMINALS

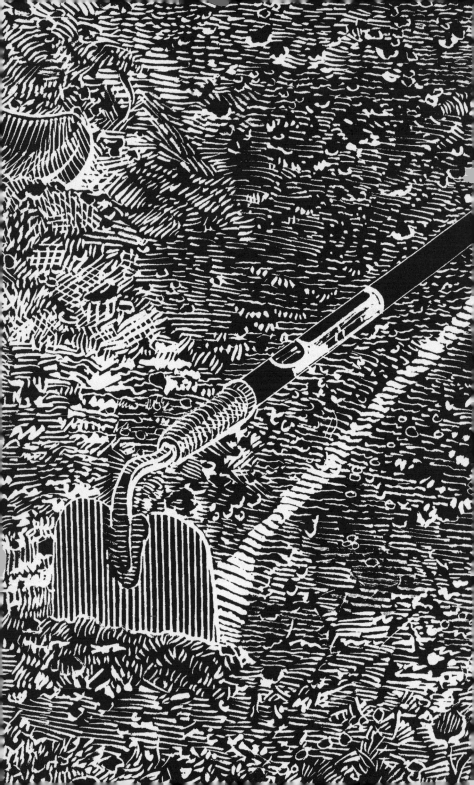

PITIFUL CRIMINALS

BY GREG BOTTOMS

DRAWINGS BY W. DAVID POWELL

COUNTERPOINT PRESS
BERKELEY

Library of Congress Cataloging-in-Publication Data
Bottoms, Greg.
Pitiful criminals / Greg Bottoms ; art by W. David Powell.
pages cm
ISBN 978-1-61902-311-6
1. Family violence. 2. Victims of family violence. 3. Violence.
4. Mentally ill offenders. I. Title.
HV6626.B676 2014
364.3—dc23
2013044918

Book design and illustration by W. David Powell

COUNTERPOINT
1919 Fifth Street
Berkeley, CA 94710
www.counterpointpress.com

Printed in the United States of America
Distributed by Publishers Group West

10 9 8 7 6 5 4 3 2 1

I was developing a tabloid sensibility. Crime jazzed me and scared me in roughly equivalent measure. My brain was a police blotter.

—James Ellroy

The sad truth is that most evil is done by people who never make up their minds to be good or evil.

—Hannah Arendt

Never make anything up—trust life.

—Wladimir Kaminer

I just want to go away and look at people and think.

—Sherwood Anderson

CONTENTS

A MESSAGE FROM PRISON

I received an email from a Department of Corrections
social worker in 2008. She had a message for me from
my older brother, Michael. He wanted contact with
his family after fifteen years in a prison psychiatric
treatment facility, to which he had been sentenced after
trying unsuccessfully to murder my mother, father, and
younger brother in an arson attempt at our home in
suburban Tidewater, Virginia.

In February 1992, in the early morning dark, he had
dismantled the house's smoke detectors, poured gas
around the garage and through the downstairs hallway,
and thrown matches into the black puddles, igniting
wood, drywall, and carpet. He then rode off on my
mother's cobwebbed, blue Sears bicycle. He had once
been a handsome, fit, quick-witted boy, but by then
he was a bloated, ashtray-smelling, deranged, yellow-
toothed twenty-five-year-old.

A couple of hours after setting the fire, he rode back
home. My ill father and younger brother were sitting on
the bumper of an ambulance. My mother, dressed in a
nightgown and jacket, was crying and shivering in the
cold as the firemen extinguished the last embers in the
smoldering garage and the police collected evidence.
Michael asked her what was for breakfast. Could they
maybe go to Denny's?

When the cops wanted to put handcuffs on him—loose,
for comfort, *just one of those procedures the manual*

insists upon, Michael—my brother figured that would be okay. He sat in the back of the police car, smiling as blue and red light sprinted around the neighborhood, flashing across the sleep-softened faces of our neighbors. He laughed. He'd really done it this time.

My brother is a paranoid schizophrenic. He used to
spend much of his time reading and writing in his
King James Bible, in which he found coded messages
and directions about his own life. Religious delusion,
across cultures and belief systems, is a common form
that auditory and visual hallucinations take in cases
of acute paranoid schizophrenia. This is because the
schizophrenic seeks salvation from his suffering the
way a person drowning seeks a gulp of air. Religion is
the road map most available for this mission—a set
system of archetypes, story lines, and metaphors aimed
at deepest human meaning, hope in bottomless despair,
and orientation within one's own mind and experience.
As the anthropologist Clifford Geertz once wrote, "Man
cannot live in a world he does not understand." When
we lose touch with so-called reality, we don't disappear
into a void of meaninglessness; we reconstitute fact,
experience, belief, and feeling into an alternate reality.
We leave the socially acceptable level of delusion we all
live in as citizens of the modern, information-glutted,
wisdom-and-knowledge-starved world and enter a
mental house of mirrors. We go "mad."

In mental illness, faith and spirituality can be elixirs
for suffering, but they can also be unhealthy and even
dangerous obsessions, especially when those in the
throes of psychosis refuse to believe they are ill, as do
about fifty percent of schizophrenics. And sometimes
these obsessions spill over into uncontrolled dementia
and, as in my brother's case, rage, criminal behavior,
and violence.

He used to pray loudly in pizza parlors, or at the food court in the mall, while the Christmas shoppers walked quickly by. He felt an otherworldly power roiling through his bones and blood and skin. Clouds had messages. A drop in temperature could carry hidden meaning. He believed there were demons in our house, under his bed, which he once tearfully told my mother about, sending her heartbeat into the red zone. He was convinced that my father, who was dying of cancer, almost dead, was a mystical and nefarious presence. The night he set the fire, he needed to burn out the evil—all very simple, really, the furthest thing from "random" violence. In his mind it was a necessary and even *unavoidable* act of destruction. Given his circumstances—evil in the house, unbearable oppression from mysterious forces, the buzzing and eye-twitching need to survive this pain—what choice did he have?

I was twenty-one in 1992, at college forty miles away
from our home the night of the incident. I am the
only one in my family to finish college, a scholarship
and fellowship kid, and it was very important to my
parents that I succeed, that I become a person with
opportunities in his life rather than dead ends. They
did what they could to protect me from my brother,
and I owe them more than I can pay. Though I have
always been quite academically average outside of
the humanities, I was a shining star to them. I later
graduated with a degree in English and journalism. I
went on to get two graduate degrees in literature and
writing. I have written books, all autobiographical and
documentary, whether fiction or nonfiction, all driven by
my layman's interest in abnormal psychology and social
psychology, in the creative mind that seeks healing and
the criminal mind bent on mayhem and destruction,
in how we—as individuals, as a society, as cultures
and subcultures—construct and perceive notions of
truth about ourselves and the strange and sometimes
dehumanizing world around us. My first book—the
darkest, the saddest—is a story about my brother's
illness. I haven't read it since going through the
publisher's galleys in 2000. I've thought about reading
it, because people still mention it to me. But I never do.

The less-selfish half of me has always wanted to help my brother, or at least help people understand his illness, its effects on sufferers, on families, on society. In the essays and stories I was trying to write back in the nineties—guided especially by books like Michael Herr's *Dispatches* and James Agee's *Let Us Now Praise Famous Men*, by the writings of George Orwell and Joan Didion and James Baldwin—I hoped that maybe a high level of prose craft could wield some power on behalf of consciousness-raising, activism, and progress. I wanted to do something like what Jack London did in *People of the Abyss*, only instead of descending into the late-Victorian world of urban poverty, I'd submerge myself in the alternate American reality of criminal behavior, criminal impulse, criminal insanity, and then, by story's end, emerge into the light of sense, understanding. But, to be honest, the selfish half of me wanted my brother, by the time of the fire, disappeared, even dead; or I wanted him to have never existed. The level of stress he caused in my family felt like someone had set a grenade on our kitchen table and then asked us, my family, to carry on with life as usual.

When Michael was gone, incarcerated in a psych ward after the fire, which itself followed dozens of smaller violent and strange episodes, including admitting to a rape and murder he did not commit, which I'll get to in a later chapter, I felt myself rising toward light and air. I could work, study. I could have friends, lovers, could get married, have a family. If I could forget him, even for a few minutes, time in my life began to flow perhaps more like time in your life. I could calm down. I could read a book. I could think. I could be less depressed.

Very few problems nowadays strike me as big compared to the problem of severe mental illness and crime in my family, in my childhood home, which went on for more than a decade, each year a little, or a lot, worse than the prior. My parents essentially had a part-time job trying to get help for my brother—new meds with toxic side effects, a treatment center that insurance would only pay for with the correct paperwork, and that only for thirty days. Then there was their need to prove, over and over, that he was in fact a danger to himself and others.

Has he hurt anyone? asked the voice on the other end of the line.

Technically, no, said my mother, but...

If there hasn't been an incident, continued the voice, and there is no police report..., etc.

My parents came from humble beginnings and little means, what John Berger once called "survival culture," which cherishes tradition and the past and views the present as a place for practical acts that ensure comfort in the here and now, rather than a place to dream of the future, to fantasize, as the present so often is for me. They had ingrained in them the working-class value of ultimately trusting and deferring to any and

all hierarchical authority—medical, legal, psychiatric—
even if that authority was faceless, bureaucratic,
harried, and barely competent. But one thing I learned
during nine years of university education was that
most experts only know what they're talking about
half the time, and that our most advanced forms of
knowledge are highly provisional, often shown to be
naïve just days or years or decades after they seemed
like breakthroughs. We look back in time and we see
barbarians. When the future looks back on us, it will
be the same. There is, I think, a deeper existence going
on always beneath the identity-shaping chaos of our
time, our culture. Call it God, or Nature, or Love, or
Stillness, or Connection. It doesn't matter what we call
it. Anyway, we barely know a thing.

The social worker wrote in the email that my brother was lonely, isolated—as I imagined every prisoner was, as I *knew* every sufferer of his disease is, especially at his level of severity, because they are stuck in darkness, pain, and slippery realities. He was also "rarely any better" and often confrontational and uncooperative. My brother is a worst-case scenario. There are many like him in our prisons and on the streets—by some estimates I've seen, up to 300,000 in the United States, but I'm going to unscientifically tell you that those estimates are *way* too low and it is probably more like double that, at least. If you live in a city, you see several people suffering from severe mental illness every day you pass by a congregation of the homeless (they would be quickly rounded up in the suburbs), and as politicians (large percentages of whom live in gated communities in those suburbs) continue to destroy what is left of the social safety net, this will only increase. "Community support"—a popular phrase in mental health care—can be a euphemism for abandonment for both the sufferer and his or her loved ones. Laws regarding treatment, driven by upside-down fiscal concerns, are passed by people with no visceral connection to the problem. Let them be faced with the choice of housing a dangerously ill loved one or putting him on the street to starve, commit crimes out of desperation, or become a victim of mind-altering violence and abuse. What would you choose? Let him stand with a phone to his head, crying for an hour while on hold, listening to Muzak with one ear and the desperate prayers of a child with the other.

My brother has, I think, erased any guilt he may
have felt for his prior deeds, or rather his crimes have
been subsumed under his ongoing hallucinations and
delusions, his anger and self- and world-loathing. His
imprisonment was undoubtedly seen by him as part
of a deep religious conspiracy, as everything was. The
social worker informed me he had almost killed himself
(he attempted suicide when I was a teenager and again
when I was in my early twenties, so I wasn't shocked)
by drinking enough water, gallons and gallons and
gallons, some of it out of toilets, to cleanse himself of his
medications, which he hates because of the side effects,
and which he was forced by law to take as part of an
"involuntary psychiatric commitment" every 180 days
because he would not take them otherwise. The social
worker and her team kept my brother from the dangers
of the larger prison—potential rape, violent attacks,
various types and levels of enslavement, and illegal
trade—by going through the rigmarole of paperwork
every six months to make sure he was medicated and in
the psychiatric unit where he belonged. He drank the
water, you could say, as a search for God beneath the
tranquilizing chemicals. God—his notion of God—was
his only hope. By chugging the water, he rid himself of
electrolytes and vitamins and minerals to the point of
seizure. So he ended up in the infirmary, handcuffed
and, I imagine, raging once his strength was back. I
remember that rage, how impossible he was to be near,
how dangerous one minute, how sad and pathetic and
tearful the next. I remember how much I loved him,

how there was a past, like a dream, before all this. I
remember how much I hated him.

I told the social worker I could not speak to him, nor
could my mother, a woman in her sixties, living a
peaceful life after many years of a damn difficult one.
Call me cold, but our problem—his problem, but ours
by extension—was intractable. I wish I had some kind
of easy prescription—something to do with politics and
policy, with therapeutic philosophies or biochemical
treatment protocols. I wish I could trust in some
earthly authority, *any* authority, but my experience of
authorities has always been a letdown, to say the least.
We barely know a thing.

The mystery of mental anguish, of the mind on the outs
with itself to the point of violence, of a version of hell
made manifest in a suburban living room, has been the
one thing in my life that has brought me to the point
where my only option seemed to be to pray, and then,
later, to look carefully at life, both present and past, to
write life down, to turn these confusing bits of reality
into the ephemeral meanings of stories.

To reengage my brother would have been suicidal. What
choice did I have? The past came flooding back. I cut
him loose to survive.

THE MINISTER'S HANDYMAN

She had been a disc jockey with her own morning show on one of the big stations in Tidewater, Virginia. A great voice, fans would later say. A real professional, they would add. She had a classical command of elocution, which she effortlessly bent into a rock 'n' roll delivery, husky and lived-in, a little weathered, worldly. She had worked hard to achieve her position in radio, but for some reason, three weeks before it happened, she quit the best gig she'd ever had. Folks speculated about a soured relationship, a lost pregnancy, maybe depression. But she was dead before anyone found out exactly why she quit.

I remember her killer. He had a voice like an air bubble purged through a rusty spigot, all scratchy throat and hard, guttural wheeze. He had bristle-like red hair and bad teeth, and whenever I used to see him—or what I remember about him now, these many years later—is that he would smile in a way that you could see the struggle he was going through to keep his top lip from rising up like a stage curtain and revealing those yellow and black—those sharply crooked—choppers. I remember kids in my city said he killed dogs and cats, that he and his brother were caught in the woods "doing it" to each other—which I heard about before I knew what "doing it" referred to. I think there was a grain of truth in the gossip about him. Maybe a little more than a grain.

Since I'm putting this together from old news articles and scant facts, let's speed up the narrative cause-and-effect, forego *mimesis* for a little *diegesis*, and say she was "going through something," and that's why she quit her job and was spending so much time tending her garden for those three jobless weeks. The garden was a rented plot of land in a Hampton city park. She grew tomatoes, cucumbers, okra, green beans, and peppers. She went there every morning, not long after dawn, when it was quiet and peaceful. And she parked every morning in the same parking lot, so if you were watching her, stalking her, or if you were a person like him on the lookout for a lone woman, she was as consistent as a clock, as solitary as a second hand. I'm sure he thought she was asking for it, alone and working and sweating like that. As he watched her, he kept his lips closed tight over his teeth, as if she could see them from her position fifty yards away, bent over her rows of vegetables, possibly thinking about the reasons she quit her job. He always imagined people were thinking about him, and thinking the very worst things, judging him, the way neighbors and teachers and cops had done throughout his entire life.

I knew him, in a way, like all the kids in my middle and
high schools knew him, the way one knows a dubious
story or legend or myth. He spoke to me a few times—
"Move" or "What are you looking at, asshole?"—and
each time a pulse of fear thumped in my temples. He
was infamous, his family was infamous. Once, so a story
I've heard goes, he and his brother and his father got
into a fight at the trailer park where they lived on the
edge of the city, along a muddy, foul-smelling creek.
They had been drinking, even though the boys were
only teenagers (both were functioning alcoholics by
the time they were fourteen, as were a number of kids
I knew back then). Someone said something, brother
insulted brother, something like that. Fists thrown.
Chairs hurled. The father, as the fight escalated, ended
the night, or ended the part of the night before the
police lights went slinging around the trailer park, by
running one of the sons over with his old Ford truck.
But somehow he—whomever got run over—just ended
up bruised and battered. The cops were called, but
everyone was okay, no one needed to go to the hospital,
so no charges were filed. The father said that yes, he
did want to kill his son there for a moment, fucker
deserved to have his head ripped off, but now he was
over that feeling and just felt like having another
beer and going to bed. The cops in my city did not like
to waste time on paperwork when this sort of family
squabbled, even if they did so nearly to the death.

Another time I saw him and his brother beat a kid
nearly to death in the woods outside of our high

school, which was uncannily like the high school in
Richard Linklater's great film *Dazed and Confused*—
knee to face, head to tree, boot stomps on the sternum,
air out of the victim's mouth like the sound of slow
shredding paper. I was maybe fourteen or fifteen.
I only saw a moment of that fight, if you could call
it that ("assault" would be a better word), walking
quickly toward a parking lot, trying to get out of there
and not to see it or be a part of it. But even so, later at
home, I wretched up a little of my cowardice and the
memory of all that blood.

Just before and then after the murder, before he was apprehended, a local minister, a trusting man who tried to see the best in people, housed him for several weeks without knowing he was guilty. The minister hired him as the new church handyman. He did odd jobs for a room and minimal pay. He was only in his early twenties, and the minister believed the job would help him both practically and spiritually. The minister later spoke up for his handyman, told the police he was a decent young man in many ways, not the monster they would assume, at least not all the time. He told them the handyman had come to God and turned his back, or tried to turn his back, on his wicked ways—most of them. And I believe that is true, that the handyman, once he had murdered, was struggling mightily those days, working at the church, to stop being who he was, a kid and then a man from a family of criminals—cursed, doomed, almost sentenced from birth to cause destruction and then be destroyed, to spend his life in jail or die early (thus not worth the cops' paperwork unless a real citizen was involved). Both the minister and the handyman believed in original sin and they believed in the devil and they believed in fate, which were not good things to believe in, really, when all evidence from your past pointed to the worst possible outcome.

At first, the handyman told the minister he had never seen the woman, said it was just horrible what had happened. But the minister noticed one day how he, the handyman, was going to the 7-Eleven and buying the morning paper and keeping up with all the stories that were being published in the days after the rape and murder, after the ex–disc jockey was found on the edge of a ditch near the public gardens where she went every morning for some peace and quiet. The church was very near to the gardens. The minister had noticed his handyman's nervousness lately. The handyman's facial expression, from morning to night, whether he was repainting old radiators or weed whacking around the gray metal fence by the playground, was "What? Me?" A curious way to look, the minister thought. The minister began spending time standing at church windows and watching his handyman. It appeared to the minister as if the handyman was waiting for cop cars to pull into the parking lot. The handyman looked at every vehicle that passed. Odd.

The handyman had thrown some dirt over the top of
the dead DJ in a rushed and abandoned attempt to hide
the body. The minister, once he began thinking about
it through sleepless nights, once the pieces started
coming together, imagined the morning of the murder,
the morning the handyman came back to the church.
He would have been sweating, his boots covered in rich
gardening dirt, one small scratch across his neck, near
his jugular vein, all of which *could* have been innocent
and explainable but seemed less and less likely to be so.
It was a pitiful crime committed by a pitiful criminal—a
sexual impulse followed through with extreme violence.
The handyman killed the woman, the paper reported,
with her own hoe.

The minister, one night after watching the chief of police make a plea for any information about the rape and murder on the local five o'clock news, went to his new handyman above the rectory and asked him about the crime. The minister felt God with him. He was not nervous. The two men sat on the cot, the one piece of furniture in the room. Did you do it, son? The minister found out almost immediately that the handyman had raped and then beaten the woman with his bare fists and, finally, to finish the job—she fought and she was very hard to kill—with her favorite gardening hoe. The minister also found out—because he was a patient listener—that it all happened as if in a dream, a fit of horrible impulse and rage the handyman could not control. He learned that the handyman had been—this will not surprise you—molested as a child, but his world was so upside down and dangerous he had never thought of it as abuse—he thought of it as normal. The handyman had been doing so well, too, he told the minister while choking back sobs, tears streaming down his face, and he liked working for the minister at the church, fixing things, mowing the lawn. He liked being in the church, a very special place, because he believed that maybe God could help him to not be who he was, whom he had been made into, an animal of sorts—that's how he saw himself sometimes, as a predator with jagged, rotting teeth—given to fits of blind, senseless rage and then immense, almost suicidal sorrow over whatever it was he had done. He said he could control himself most of the time, but every once in a while something overcame him, something he had started to believe was the devil. He told the minister that there was nothing he would like better than to stay in the room above the rectory, to be able to sleep on his cot at night and listen to the minister preach on Sunday about the ways of sin and the possibility of redemption, and then work through the week painting and repairing and thinking about God and the minister's message. The minister, in a calm voice, told the handyman that unfortunately that was no longer possible.

I think the minister was in great danger at this point—the moment of the confession, I mean. He had a murderer and rapist in his church, a desperate and defeated man unable to control his rage, a sick and sharp-toothed predator, a man with the evil some call the devil inside him, coiled to spring forth. Anything could have happened. But the minister put his hand on the hand of the handyman and he suggested that they pray together for guidance, which they did. The minister promised the handyman that he would help him, would walk him to the police station, which was not far from the city garden or the church, where the handyman could make his confession, a confession to the police but also a confession before God, who was the only one, the minister said, who had the power to forgive him.

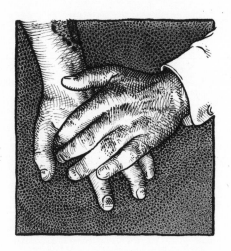

In the years after that, the minister spoke to the handyman once a month or so in prison and would conduct a bible study with him over the phone. During these bible study sessions the minister would recite excerpts from his sermons from the previous month of Sundays. This was a promise the minister had made to the handyman, a condition of the handyman turning himself in. The minister was sickened in his soul by the whole ordeal, of course he was, he was human after all, but he had made a promise and would keep it. And he would carry on and keep up appearances. He was a man of the cloth. He was a man of his word.

After the trial, the minister started his own plot at the community garden, which was another promise he had made and kept—but this one only to himself—and every morning he worked for an hour on what would become impressive and bountiful rows of vegetables, almost all of which he gave to homeless shelters and the neediest people in his congregation. After gardening each morning, the minister went to the ditch, to the very spot where his former handyman and tenant had raped and murdered the ex–disc jockey, and said a prayer for the woman, for the murderer, and especially for himself, because after the crime he became secretly filled with doubt about whether people, capable of such evil deeds and such naiveté about the evil in others, were not culpable beyond God's forgiveness.

THE SHOOTER

The shooter came through the burgundy double-doors
of a Virginia Baptist church, an enormous, brick
megachurch on the corner of a busy intersection. A
beautiful day—sunny, breezy, warm but not hot. She
wore a sea-foam-green dress, her long black hair rolled
up into a bun, pinned to the back of her head. She was
part of a wedding procession. I had to be dreaming.

A deliveryman at the time, a legal courier, I had stopped
at a red light by the megachurch, which took up part
of a city block along my regular Thursday route. It was
locally famous for its charismatic pastor and the many
hundreds it packed in every Sunday.

The procession of about fifteen well-dressed women and
men—a rehearsal, I assumed—made its way along a
sidewalk by the busy street. When they stopped and
turned to face the church's double doors, where they
would be positioned to acknowledge the forthcoming
newlyweds during a Saturday ceremony, the shooter
was smiling. Then she laughed, a deep, joyful laugh. She
hugged one of the four other girls lined up beside her,
also in sea-foam-green dresses.

I'd heard the rumors, the gossip. Had read the newspaper articles, seen the television news coverage of the
shooting and trial. For years I'd wondered about the
shooter's fate. For years she'd occupied some part of my
thoughts. Here she was, a bridesmaid.

On a cold, gray weekday afternoon in February 1985, my childhood friend Sammy, fifteen, and two other boys, fourteen and fifteen, entered the shooter's home.

The shooter, seventeen, and her sister, thirteen, lived in a small, brick rancher on a quarter acre lot on a street of similar houses.

Sammy "liked" the shooter's sister. The sister, according to the boys' story at the trial, invited the boys in about an hour after our high school had let out. For some reason the boys could not agree on during questioning, she then decided they should leave.

The three boys stood at the side door, just inside the house, in a space that doubled as a laundry room and a closet for the shooter's father's hunting jackets, shoes, and boots.

Instead of leaving, two of the boys, maybe Sammy (it's not clear in the newspaper articles), went up a steep set of stairs, almost a ladder, in the back of the room, which led to an attic/storage space.

The shooter's sister laughed, according to the boys.

She was not—also according to the boys—angry.

There was no indication of what was to come.

The shooter then came into the laundry room with her

father's .22 pistol, which was loaded and kept in the
drawer of his night table, within arm's reach of where
he slept. She said she had a bullet for everyone and then
one for herself.

The two boys had come down the steep stairs by now
and Sammy said to put the gun down. He held up his
hands, deeply afraid, as anyone would be, of being shot.
He said, I can get you in big trouble, which was the last
thing he said.

The shooter took aim and, teeth clenched, pulled the
trigger, sending, in a fraction of a second, a bullet
through Sammy's flesh and skull and into his brain,

where it would stay until a medical examiner removed it forcefully with large, sterilized pincers.

Sammy dropped like a bag of sand to the concrete floor, a puddle of black-looking blood spreading quickly away from his head. The shooter's sister, after about thirty seconds of expanding and insane silence, screamed. She screamed and screamed. She screamed so loud and long she lost her voice and could not answer the police's questions until the next day.

The shooter locked herself in her room with the gun.

The boys ran from the house.

A neighbor called the police.

These are the basic facts, as best as I can gather them, of the boys' story.

The shooter's sister, at the trial, had a different story. She started her version of what happened, of how the shooting transpired, earlier in the day. She remembered walking out of school, toward her bus. Sammy approached her. He was on the way to his friend's car, because Sammy was cool and cool kids, once they were fifteen or sixteen, didn't ride the bus. He said he wanted to come over so they could finish what they had started. He was talking about how he and the shooter's sister had kissed the Friday before at a "party"—a kid's house where a dozen young teens sat around drinking beer to the edge of, or just beyond, puking.

The shooter's sister said she was busy. She regretted kissing Sammy; she wouldn't have done it had she not chugged a warm beer in less than a minute. Sammy was a sketchy creep. She wasn't "into him." She wouldn't *give in to peer pressure* and drink like that again. Not ever. She was only going to hang out with her church friends. The boys around town—me included—were losers.

Sammy said he would see her later.

Over her shoulder, she said she was serious, and not to bug her. She had loads of homework.

Sammy laughed, because Sammy and I and most of the kids I hung around did not do homework (I actually did do homework, but pretended I did not).

After school, at home, the shooter's sister sat down to study at the kitchen table, which she did until her mom and dad got home from their jobs—Dad from the local shipyard (where my father also worked), Mom from I don't know.

There was a knock at the side door, just through the laundry room adjacent the kitchen: Sammy and his two friends.

The shooter's sister flung open the door and said she couldn't hang out.

Sammy said sure, okay, as he stepped into the laundry room, his two friends behind him.

The shooter's sister told them to leave. She did not—absolutely did not—invite them in.

But none of the boys made a move to leave; one of the other two boys shut the side door behind them.

Sammy either touched or took hold of the shooter's sister's arms. She said something like stop, don't touch me, you have to leave.

The shooter came into the laundry room. She said something like what do you want, leave, get out.

Then one of the boys mentioned the stairs. Two of them went up. Maybe Sammy. One made a suggestive

comment about how nice and dark it was up there.
Maybe Sammy.

The shooter left the room.

The shooter's sister said to get out now. Right now.

The shooter rushed back into the laundry room with
her father's .22. She said she had a bullet for each boy
and then one for herself, yes, she did say that, but
she was only kidding because she thought it wasn't
loaded. Everything happened so fast, the shooter's
sister later said, when she had a voice again, when
she wasn't screaming.

The two boys came down the steep stairs—slowly—and
Sammy said to put the gun down. He held up his hands,
deeply afraid—as anyone would be—of being shot. I can
get you in big trouble, he said, which was the last thing
he said.

The shooter pulled the trigger. Sammy collapsed as if
his skeleton had instantly disintegrated. He fell so fast
and hard it didn't seem real. It wasn't exactly like a
movie, but it wasn't like life either. It was worse than
both, worse, one of the boys there would later say, than,
like, anything. The shooter and her sister, for about five
seconds—the five seconds it took for the blood to start to
visibly spread—thought Sammy was joking; he was like
that. The gun, after all, wasn't even loaded. She didn't
believe it, then she did, then she screamed.

The shooter's story was factually the same as her sister's, since it is a lawyer's job to get everyone on one side of a trial to agree on details and one essential narrative truth, which in this case was that the shooting had been a tragic accident, an awful, deadly mistake, but definitely not second-degree murder and worth a twenty-five-to-life sentence. Our legal system does not reward absolute veracity, if you believe in such a thing. It rewards the soundest argument within the context of the malleable facts of any potentially criminal situation.

The shooter—like Sammy and my other friends—didn't usually do homework. She watched TV after school, mostly soap operas, where emotions were outsized, where men and women cried and betrayed each other and sometimes killed one another and kept terrible secrets, even from themselves, secrets that ultimately would eat them from inside and destroy them, unless they chose, in some final act, a different and more righteous and true path and found redemption, found Jesus or something that might function within an individual's life the way Jesus is supposed to, like an exceptional exercise plan, or antidepressants.

This lover of soap operas, the shooter, was unpopular, about as despised as a person can be in a mediocre Virginia public high school. Imagine a person people walk away from and don't listen to and talk about cruelly when she leaves a space. Imagine if every interaction you had with another human being suggested you were lesser, an ugly, filthy, useless thing. Imagine if every expression sweeping past you in the school hallways—a school that you hated but were forced by law to go to—came lit with repugnance, repudiation, and disgust. That's how it was for the shooter.

She had a learning disability and was in remedial classes. But she understood, though it took her until puberty to really figure it out, that people did not like her, not at all. Once she understood this—and those interactions and expressions are powerful communicators but are not concrete enough to be "evidence"—she began to be shaped by that understanding. The disliked person, the most disliked person—that's who she was. Trying out her persona of loser, of waste case, she would stare at people, steal small items like calculators and pens, laugh too loudly and at the wrong time, bump smaller girls, talk about menstruation and God, about suicide or murder. This made it seem as though *she* was the one who had decided to have everyone not like her. It was *her* choice. Her life, her identity in the community, was fully in her power to control.

The shooter heard the commotion in the laundry room. She heard her sister shout get out. She got up from in front of the TV, from watching a show where perhaps a female character was on trial for murder after killing her abusive husband, who was, of course, *representative* of so much male insult and abuse, all the crap she had to deal with. She went to the laundry room. She said for the boys to leave or else, she did say that, but even that, she said at the trial, was a joke. The boys were joking. She was joking. But they wouldn't leave, the stupid boys. Why wouldn't they just leave?

So she thought she would scare them, teach them a lesson. Don't be the abusive husband. Don't look at me like that. Don't talk about me behind my back. Don't mess with my smart, pretty, not-yet-totally-defeated sister.

She left and came back with her father's gun. She didn't know it was loaded, she swore, and her father, in tears, later said he rarely kept it loaded. She pointed it at Sammy's head after he came down from the attic (or didn't). Sammy said to put that down. He held up his hands, deeply afraid—as anyone would be—of being shot. He said, I can get you in big trouble, which was the last thing he said.

(During the trial, and maybe after, I don't know, the shooter said she had no memory of what happened next. A bang, like a metal hammer hitting concrete in an empty room, her ears ringing, and then talking to her crying mom and dad in the police station a couple of hours later. Time vanished. And it was easy to find experts who could attest to the fact that this is common around traumatic experience. The mind blanks. Slowly, over time, it shapes and reshapes that experience, with memory and imagination, into something rational and understandable, tolerable—in her case the shooting was, and forever had to be, a mistake, not exactly like something she watched on TV but as similar to that passive viewing experience as to anything she had known in real life, in a here, in a now.)

She pulled the trigger. That's a fact common to every story about the shooting. And a bullet exited her father's pistol, which she either knew or did not know was loaded, and went into my old friend's head, killing him.

At the wake, which hundreds of people attended (it was an *American high school shooting* and a minor media event), Sammy's mother slowly—over the course of hours—became agitated, manic, and then hysterical, unhinged in her grief—wild-eyed, shaggy-haired, disheveled in her dress—as if she'd been plugged into a thousand volts. She had to be taken to a back room. She had a ghost in her brain, her beloved lost child, blocking out everything we call life.

Sammy's father, on the other hand, often had his head down, as if he were looking at people's shoes, as if he needed desperately to sleep, but then he would perk up and thank people for coming and wish them well, like maybe this wasn't a wake at all, or at least not one so directly connected to him. Over time, I think the mother fared better. She became less charged, as you would expect, but he became more and more tired, exhausted in his very soul. His boy. All through the wake and the funeral, after he looked up from people's shoes and shook their hands, this phrase: "My boy. My boy."

The shooter received a five-year suspended sentence for involuntary manslaughter. There was no way to prove she knew the gun was loaded. She had the better lawyer, the better story, and as I said, the process of law is the process of storytelling.

After the shooting, right at first—and I was only
fourteen that winter—I wanted her to die. I did. I cried
and cried and cried. The world was senseless. The world
was shit. Me a shaved-head skateboarder: Fuck it. Fuck
you. Fuck everything.

She killed my friend. I knew he was too aggressive that
day, too sexually suggestive, but he didn't intend, nor
was he capable of, rape. I don't think so, anyway. He
might have left that place one day, our city I mean,
those neighborhoods, just gotten away, and become
an adult who regretted the way he treated some
people, who regretted the way he'd learned to think
about women as either maternal objects or sex toys,
who regretted parts of who he was, and changed. He
might have even become the kind of person capable of
examining how he acquired some of his attitudes and
perceptions about himself, about boys and girls, men
and women, sex. He might have wanted to *help* a kid
like the one he was and the one who killed him. He
might have. Maybe.

After a while, a year or so, I did not want the shooter to die anymore. I didn't want anyone to die. I wanted people to come back. Somewhere Heidegger says we are constantly tumbling towards death, and every once in a while we get a clear glimpse of this fact. We must then adjust our minds to accommodate the new knowledge. It makes us sadder, but also more urgent in our living, more aware that lives are fragile, ephemeral, not to be wished away. It makes us, it should make us, *humble*.

I decided, given the stories, given the shifting facts, the speculation about motives and intent—the rumors, the gossip, the newspaper articles, the nightly news coverage, all of it partly true, none of it *true*—to believe that she didn't mean it, she didn't know a bullet was in the chamber. Or if she did mean it, she only did so in the tenth of a second it took her to kill Sammy, for which she should—it was only a tenth of a second—be forgiven.

As I edged ahead in traffic the day I saw her, off to my next stop, I watched the shooter in her new life, among friends, at a wedding rehearsal, smiling. Since the shooting, I had seen her once, outside an abandoned skating rink, maybe five years before. She had been with a group of boys, locally famous thugs—greasy, long-haired, tattooed. She had worn her criminal record proudly then, a big middle finger to the world, because I doubt she knew what else to do with it—her criminal record, her middle finger, the world. Later, I heard, she pulled out half of her hair, became afraid people were watching her house, bugging her phone, and she was institutionalized. And still later, according to rumor, she survived a suicide attempt, got clean from drugs and alcohol, got on antidepressant medication, and got a job. That's when she joined the megachurch. She accepted Christ into her life and was born again.

Believe what you will, but who can doubt the power
of a full-hearted acceptance of those two words—born
again—to shift the meaning of a person's life? What is
magic if not a belief in the truth of magic? What is your
life if not an organized, believable story about your life?
What is suffering and anguish if not the loss of this
story? Who has grown into adulthood and not wished, at
some point, to be born again?

I imagine the shooter wept so hard on the day she found God her whole body quaked, for she had never believed, not even for a second, that a sinner like her, a killer like her, a person as confused, dehumanized, and ruined as her, could be saved.

SCARFACE

Later, when he was at his parents' opulent home along the James River convalescing—lucky to be alive, his once-handsome face cobbled back together like a jigsaw puzzle—he couldn't believe it started with the pizza delivery guy. How brash and careless and stupid could he have been? His big mouth. And the *pizza* guy.

He was a kid from the upper class, from a family of multi-named Virginia aristocrats. Something something something, Jr. Something something something, III. Money was never a problem. A black sheep, he wanted, in high school, to be a black *kid*, or at least his mass-mediated notion of a street-tough black kid, so he balked at all the pressure to be upstanding and successful like his siblings, to carry forth the family name and crest (yes, they even had a crest) into science, engineering, medicine, local politics.

Everyone in his family had gone to the same private school, a Southern version of Choate or Exeter, which he hated. The other kids in blue or pink button-up polo shirts. The Volvos and Mercedes and expensive soccer backpacks. Virginia blue bloods with names like Tiffany and Ashley, James and Chaz, all overly concerned with grades and extracurricular resume stuffers, all hoping to get accepted to William & Mary, UVA, George Washington, Georgetown, where their moms or dads went.

He liked hanging with the Newport News city kids, whom his parents considered riffraff, *highly dysfunctional*. He liked skateboarding at the halfpipe, sharing their stolen liquor in the woods, talking about sex, drugs, music, fighting. Beat the hell out of homework and track practice.

His parents—busy professionals with no clue what their kid was up to all day and why he was such a screw-up—finally gave in and let him go to the public city high school (since he was bombing at private school), where his new friends sat in the back of classrooms drawing dicks on the desks and smoked joints in the bathroom during lunch, the teachers smelling the smoke and walking by because they didn't want any trouble—slashed tires or late-night phone threats. Kids ruled the public school. The place was dangerous, Darwinian. He loved it.

He started smoking *a lot* of pot, before school, after school, dreaming his way down the lockered halls, then he got into cocaine, started to idolize the idea of the gangster. He figured he'd buy pot, smoke some, sell the rest, and then use the profits he made plus his plush allowance for the coke. Worked pretty well. Gave him a taste of the business end of things.

He was naturally smart, and his public school was such a joke academically, the bar set so low, that he could do almost nothing and make A's. Turning in homework was miraculous beyond a teacher's hope. Bringing the right books to class was A- seriousness. He skated through. He applied to college. He knew the party would be *way* better there. He was accepted to a few schools, but none of the ones his parents hoped for, nothing big-name public or Ivy League, which didn't interest him anyway. He chose a posh, crazy-expensive private college in the deep South known for its average academics, pretensions, and partying. His idea of college: booze, drugs, women. Learn squat. Pick up a degree at the end. Let the awesomeness begin!

College was even better than he thought—all of it except the classes. The professors were real scholars who *expected* engagement from the students—participation, intellectual attention, rigor, seriousness. He couldn't even get the punctuality part right, sleeping until noon most days. Still, the parties *raged*. He was on academic probation in just one semester, close to going home for good, booted, but after that scare he buckled down enough to keep the C average he needed to not get kicked out.

Freshman year was good for meeting people. He was handsome and trendy-fashionable and super-social, especially when a little buzzed, drunk or high or both, which was all the time, so he became the center of the first-year party scene. He started dealing a little weed, though he didn't need the money because the blue-blood parents back in Virginia ("the 'rents back in Vah," as he would say) paid all the bills. He did it because…because he'd watched *Scarface* fifty times and because he tried to talk like a black gangbanger from Baltimore or Richmond even though he grew up in a mansion on a historic Virginia river. He wasn't just white; he was like the history of Southern whiteness in an Atlanta Braves hat. He reveled in the rush of being—he smiled when he said this—a *criminal*. He did it, the dealing, because he was by no means unique, because he was a certain kind of American kid. Crime movies + first-person shooter video games + sadistic, egomaniacal rap + missing parents + money + media babble + nihilism +

hedonism + drugs + porn + all-the-time-in-the-world. Privilege has its privileges, one of which is the freedom to flush your life.

Sophomore year he talked his parents into letting him move into an apartment with a roommate. That's when the steady dealing really began.

It was a jolt every time he bought the weed in minor bulk—two pounds, three pounds—from a *serious drug dealer*, whom he had met through one of his friends, a small-time seller of mostly pot and ecstasy tabs. He liked picking up dope like a real gangsta, driving it stealthily through the city, and then weighing it out into one-ounce baggies in his apartment to sell to the college crowd. Pretty soon after starting to deal, he was rolling in dough, buying drinks for all his friends at the bars, throwing parties, buying big-screen TVs and the latest video-game ware.

He was selling weed *and* smoking it, which can make you careless, lackadaisical, a person not watching your own back the way you should when you have drawers full of narcotics and cash. On weekends, party time, he did the harder stuff—ecstasy and coke mostly, but sometimes mushrooms or acid or even oxy. He was really careless then, "smoking up" near-strangers, bragging/slurring about his escapades, his cash, his connections. He was into the *celebrity* of it. He was becoming an addict and alcoholic. He felt bad only while sober. He couldn't yet see any downsides.

He garnered a reputation after a few months in the apartment. He didn't just know where the party was— he was it. This reputation spread beyond the college crowd, out into the rougher sections of the city just a few blocks away.

He thought he was Big Time. Some local elements thought he was a joke.

One weeknight, a down night with no major parties going, he and four friends sat around playing Halo and smoking cigar-sized joints. They got the munchies. Always the big spender, he suggested he spring for some pizzas.

The pizza delivery guy knocked. He was nineteen. He said what's up. He smelled the weed, said it smelled really good in there.

Magnanimous, he invited the pizza guy in to sit down, eat a piece of the pizza he had delivered, and take a few hits from the big bong on the coffee table. He bragged like an idiot about all the money he had, the cabinet full of top-shelf booze, his super top-secret major drug supplier. New video game controls!

The pizza guy told his friend, a twenty-one-year-old out on probation for burglary, about the college kid who thought he was Scarface. *Freakin' Virginia preppy, bro. Has no clue what he's doin'.*

They cased the apartment. Over the next month, the pizza guy dropped by a couple of times when he was at the apartment complex delivering pizzas and got high before going back to work. He asked a lot of questions. When did the roommate have class? Did they work at all? What was their daily schedule? Just wondering.

So one day the nineteen-year-old pizza delivery guy and
his friend, the twenty-one-year-old burglar, put on ski
masks, parked in front of the dealer's apartment before
dawn, and then went and banged on the door at 5:30 a.m.

The dealer, groggy, wearing clothes from the night
before, opened the door without looking through the
peephole, which only someone with a head full of drugs
would do.

The burglar had a sawed-off shotgun. The pizza guy
thought that was just for looks, he would later say in a
police interview.

The dealer looked at the gun. He was alone. His
roommate had stayed over at his girlfriend's. He
cooperated. He said take what you want, take it all,
no problem. And they did. They took the weed, all
the cash, some watches and bracelets, video games,
CDs, until the duffle bag they had brought in was
stuffed. The dealer was friendly the whole time,
accommodating even, trying to hide how scared he was,
trying to survive this moment. Whatever you want, he
said. Anything, he said. Take it.

But as they left, the burglar had a feeling that the
dealer knew it was the pizza guy robbing him. He'd
done some time and didn't want to do any more, would
do just about anything to avoid it. The dealer didn't say
anything to suggest that he absolutely *knew* it was the
pizza guy, but the burglar had that feeling and didn't

want to take a chance.

The burglar pointed the shotgun at the dealer's head. Fuck it. He pulled the trigger. He blew most of the dealer's face off. Skin and bone fragments and blood burst through the apartment like water from a busted fire hydrant.

The pizza guy and the burglar, thinking the dealer was dead—how could he not be?—sprinted back to their beat-up sedan and took off.

The sun was just coming up. Multiple witnesses would be able to identify the car, as well as the height, build, and skin color (white) of the ski-masked guys with the duffle bag and shotgun who took off in it.

He wasn't dead. That's the amazing thing. He wasn't even *unconscious*. The dealer ran out of the apartment, hands over what was left of his face, blood pouring from the wound. He ran to his neighbor and banged on the door. Then another neighbor. Then another. People came to the windows—they had heard the gunshot and were up, wondering where the *bang* had come from—but no one, not one person, would open their door. They didn't want to get shot. They didn't want blood all over their carpet. The dealer wanted to scream for help but he didn't have a bottom jaw or a tongue.

He ran back into his apartment, got his keys, headed for his four-wheel-drive, and somehow drove himself to the corner gas station, where he passed out in the parking lot in a puddle of blood.

I knew a guy who knew this guy. I recently went back and read all the newspaper articles about this.

After many weeks in intensive care, the dealer went back home with his parents, who were devastated, in disbelief. He never confessed to dealing drugs, and there were no drugs in his apartment when the detectives checked since they had been stolen, only a few pipes and a set of scales. He maintained that he didn't know why he was robbed and shot, and his parents believed that it was just bad luck. They never should have let him live in that apartment in that crime-ridden city. Their baby.

The two robbers, the pizza guy and the burglar, were found out and arrested within a couple weeks because they both bragged about what they'd done, flashing around cash and weed and new video games and CDs. Both received decades of jail time for robbery and attempted murder.

To this day, the ex-dealer, after many surgeries, has only parts of his face left and a slow, reconstructed tongue. I've heard he still lives and works at his parents' home, does some kind of telecommuting job with computers, tries not to let anyone see him beyond his immediate family. Avoids old acquaintances. Avoids mirrors. Doesn't talk much because it's difficult and he knows it sounds weird. Tries to forget.

In the last article that appeared about the robbery and shooting, the reporter interviewed the crime-scene clean-up supervisor. It took five hours to clean all the blood and "biological material" out of the apartment, he said. He couldn't believe that someone could lose that much blood and survive. He couldn't imagine what the poor guy must look like.

THE TRUCE

The holdup at the Kwik Pik was at an impasse. Old Frank, the cantankerous owner, said for J.T., a local criminal I knew and feared as a kid, to take his stupid mask off and put down his father's twelve-gauge shotgun.

J.T. was sixteen. He was sweating in the wool stocking cap with eyeholes coarsely cut out of the front that he was using as a mask. He told Old Frank he wasn't J.T., didn't have any idea who J.T. was, and this wasn't his dad's gun, whoever his dad even was anyway, damn it.

Now go on and get out of my store with your stupid gun, J.T., I'm serious, said Old Frank.

Not until I get the money, said J.T. And I don't know any J.T., you old bastard.

This all began weeks earlier, when Old Frank told J.T. never to come into his small, run-down convenience store again after showing up while tripping on LSD and knocking every can of Hormel chili, Libby's canned fruit, and Campbell's soup off a shelf while yelling that he was the Messiah and the food available in Kwik Pik was an insult to the temple of the body. He also said—though this part was hard to understand even for the kids who were themselves regulars with LSD—that he would not allow a place like Kwik Pik to continue to exist on this earth because the shelves stretched evilly into the grand distance of the light.

Old Frank and J.T. were the only ones in the store during the holdup (I heard this story from one of J.T.'s friends months later). They stared each other down. Old Frank didn't move toward the cash register. He would rather have a hole blown through him and his gut chunks blasted onto the back wall than give the little prick J.T. the cash from his till, never mind from his cheap safe in the back.

Old Frank's stalling was working. J.T. was getting nervous, eyes darting around like marbles rolling in the holes of the hot wool mask.

Finally—we're talking five minutes or more, which was a long time for no customers to come in—J.T. told Old Frank that he was going to have to kill him and make a run for it because that was the only way he was going to be able to stay out of jail.

Playing for his life now, Old Frank said, Wait, don't kill me because you'll regret that and be locked up forever. You'll rot in jail.

Well, what am I going to do then, Old Frank? J.T. was now almost in tears. I'm going to get into big-time trouble here, man, he said. I mean, I took my dad's gun and it's loaded and everything.

Here's what we're going to do, Old Frank said. You leave now. You go as fast as you can and run into the woods and get that mask off and go into your house through the back door, unload that gun, and put it back in your father's case just exactly the way you found it. If you do that, if you don't kill me and take my money and you do what I'm telling you, and do it as quickly as you can, I mean right now, I'll forget this little thing here between us ever happened.

Will you let me come back in here with my friends and play Donkey Kong and get a Coke and a Moon Pie? J.T. asked, seeing the wisdom in Old Frank's words.

Old Frank took a second on that one because he needed to continue to exude a little authority in this situation, a situation in which, in reality, he had no inherent authority. Finally he said, If you're not on dope and you leave my cans alone and behave yourself, you can come in, yes, but only if you leave right now and do what I told you.

J.T. left and did what Old Frank told him—ran through the woods, went into his empty house through the back, unloaded the gun, put it back in the case, and then threw the itchy wool mask into the outside garbage can.

A few weeks later, though, J.T. shot a kid running through the woods with buckshot because he really had it in his mind to shoot a person to see what that was like. The runner was more than fifty yards away and buckshot is not accurate at that distance, so he only ended up with a few pellets lodged into his neck, back, and ass. J.T. went to juvie for that one, and I never saw him again. I assume he's lived his life in and out of prisons. Or he's dead.

Old Frank lived to be almost 100 and died in a nursing home many years later. He kept his promise to J.T., who spent several afternoons after the holdup in Kwik Pik, playing Donkey Kong with his gang, drinking Cokes and eating Moon Pies, before getting locked up for shooting that kid in the woods just to see what it felt like.

ATTEMPTED MURDER MYSTERY

They seemed like a nice couple, if a little down on their luck. She looked forty, forty-five maybe, but she'd lived a hard life, so it was difficult to tell her exact age. She could have been thirty-five, thirty-two, something like that, but wind-chapped by the gale of her existence. He was in his mid-twenties. They had two kids: a boy from one of her previous two marriages—around fifteen, I'd guess—and a baby girl who was theirs. The baby was the reason they were together, in need of a place to live, trying to make the marriage work.

My wife and I, back then in 2001 and 2002, owned a century-old farmhouse on the western side of Afton Mountain in Virginia. It was just a few miles from the Appalachian Trail. Beautiful rolling country, mountains like ever-changing paintings to the east and west. My wife's vegetable and flower gardens. I loved that place.

But I'd been offered a teaching position at a small liberal arts college, which came with a free apartment if we wanted it. We had a baby son, which was a joy, a blessing, but it also twisted around our priorities, our professional lives, what we expected and needed for the future. We went from thinking about ourselves and each other to having this bundle of cooing cells and soul become the center of the known universe. Love on speed and steroids. We figured we'd take the free place while I taught as a visiting writing professor. We'd make money by renting the house. My wife wouldn't need to work for a year. Simple.

During the first few months that we were renting out our place, and living about fifty miles from it, I spoke on the phone several times to both the man and the woman about minor things—how to turn up the water heater, what to do if a pipe seemed like it was freezing, how to keep mice from coming into the cellar in the late fall, when the temperature dropped and a gray cloud bank and a relentless northwest wind sometimes pummeled the Shenandoah Valley. They were always polite in these conversations, even a little deferential. I remember laughing and joking with them, trying, no doubt, to be a likeable landlord, to erase the implicit power imbalance between us having to do with the fact that I *owned* the house; I wanted to give them the sense, at every opportunity, that I was from the working class, a writer-artist dude all about the lives and meanings of the proletariat. I was for the The People, man.

The first more serious problem occurred maybe two or three months after they'd moved in. The woman called me, nervous, not frantic, to say she smelled gas. I told her to call the gas company *immediately*. The gas company rushed out, turned off the gas, and then found a copper pipe outside the house that had been pinched and bent, creating a small hole for the gas to escape. Weird.

I met the gas guy later that same day, after driving fifty miles as soon as I finished teaching my morning class. He was heavy-set, with a balding head and a brown-red mustache, wearing a gas company button-up shirt and Carhartt jeans.

Maybe a dog or a fox or even a big, angry skunk had tried to get into the cellar—there were some cracks in the foundation emanating heat—and squeezed their way between the pipe and the house, getting stuck, wriggling free, bending the pipe, pinching it, causing the leak. That was the gas guy's best guess. A little mysterious, really, but he'd seen plenty of stranger things happen. He fixed it. I told him to bill me.

I headed for my truck, which was out in the long dirt and gravel driveway, near a small storage outbuilding. On my way, the man, my renter, came hurrying out of the house to catch me. I stopped and smiled and said sorry for the problem, the inconvenience, and that everything would be okay now. Problem fixed. Good landlord hand out for the greeting. You're welcome. But he was agitated, like a completely different person than the one who had signed the lease a few months prior and the one I'd spoken to on the phone more recently. He was tall, six foot or so, and lean and muscular from construction work. Today he looked like maybe he was on something—tiny veins in his eyes the color of garden-ripe tomatoes—but I couldn't guess what, only that it was a drug that made you nervous and big-eyed and sweaty, even though it was cold out.

He almost barked at me. He said they could have been killed, what kind of place was this? He then told me that they needed a runner on the painted wooden stairs, because his wife had fallen "two or three times" in her socks.

Because of the way he came at me, I was getting a little pissed, certainly not feeling charitable. I felt, in fact, like telling him to tell her to stop wearing slippery socks, or get some exercise and take care of herself a little better, or stop drinking, or stop taking whatever the hell he was on, since my wife and I had *never* slipped on those stairs. Were these people idiots?

Instead, composed, I said I'd talk to my wife when I got back to the college and see what we could do.

I blew off the runner request—I mean, I wasn't some posh time-share manager, and I was busy with a teaching gig and a new baby—so I thought that might be what the wife was calling about the next time, to complain about the never-appearing stair runner.

She said there was a problem. She was on the verge of tears, voice shaky, some excess snot audibly moving around.

What kind of problem?

With my husband.

Okay.

He's sick.

I'm sorry to hear that. What's wrong? You've called a doctor?

You don't understand. He's *sick*. We got married, you know, because of little Lisa, and I never really knew.

Not sure I follow.

He's sick.

Okay. Right. How?

He's messed up in his head. He hates my boy. My boy

won't be around. I don't know where he goes. It's cold.

I don't think I'm the person to call about this. Is there something going on at the house, I mean *with* the house? The gas? The heat? Rain-ruts appearing in the driveway after these storms lately?

Maybe. Maybe. I don't know. Then she hung up.

Maybe what? I wondered, but I didn't call her back because I was nearly late for a meeting already.

I couldn't sleep that night. These renters—what a nightmare. They had a six-month lease, which was up in about six weeks, and I'd already decided they were out. Gone. No amount of money was worth having people I increasingly did not trust—or even understand—in my house.

Why couldn't I sleep?

I had—I really had—what people mean when they say they have "the creeps"—an uneasy feeling, a low-grade fight-flight response. I mean anxiety, I guess. Big time. What was going on at my house? Who were these people? Was the guy some kind of meth head?

Next morning I drove the fifty miles over and through the Blue Ridge, back out to the house. I can't explain it, but I had an overwhelming feeling that I needed to go to the house, and go *now*.

I knocked. No one answered. I knocked again.

I walked around the house, *my* house, and the outside seemed okay. But then I went to check on the fixed copper gas pipe, which was shiny with bright, new stickers on it. It was—I couldn't believe it—cinched and bent again, but this time it looked like someone had tried to rip it off the outside wall. The gas smell was strong. No animal could have done this.

I ran around the house, panicked. I banged on the door again, before I dug through my jean pockets for my own keys to let myself in. This time the teenage son came to the door. He opened it wearing his old, filthy ski jacket. He was tall and skinny, with a puzzled look on his face. He said he was glad I was here because the heat stopped working again.

Before he finished his sentence, I blasted past him and into my cellar—I was very much thinking this way now: *my* cellar, *my* house—and twisted the gas valve to off, shutting everything down.

While I waited for someone from the gas company to come back out and fix the pipe, again, I stood in *my* kitchen and asked the teenage son some questions. But

he was worse even than his parents, impossible to talk to, his answer to everything "I don't know."

What happened to the pipe?

I don't know.

Any ideas?

I don't know.

Have you seen anyone outside the house, walking around?

I don't know. No. I don't know.

Where is your mother?

I don't know.

Where is your stepdad?

He's not my stepdad.

He's married to your mom, right?

That doesn't mean he is anything to me. He's *nothing* to me.

Okay. But where is he?

I don't know. I don't care.

The gas guy—the same guy—said it was "pretty fishy" to have this happen twice. Brand-new pipe, bent like this? He still thought it could be an animal, but it could be, he also thought, one of the people in the house. Twice? That was kind of odd and suspicious, yessir. If it were him, he'd keep a close eye out. Meanwhile he'd put on a stronger pipe, one you couldn't bend without serious tools.

My tenants, to the relief of my wife and I, asked to leave a few weeks early. The couple was splitting up—the mother, teenager, and baby going to live with a relative, the man going somewhere else that didn't concern me as long as it was out of *my* house. I'd already let them know I wasn't giving back the deposit, which wasn't going to cover even half of the damage I'd later find.

I went to clean up the house once they were gone,
driving the fifty miles one way several days in a row. My
hardwood floors were scratched. The stairs—those so-
called dangerously slippery stairs—were deeply gouged,
as if the dressers and beds and trunks upstairs had
been drug down by only one person, the whole weight of
each piece of furniture slamming onto every step on the
way down.

The bathrooms were filthy. Shit-stained toilets. Pubic
hair stuck to grimy toilet rims. Mould around the sinks
and faucets, in the showers and bathtubs.

Outside they'd left bags and bags of trash. I was so
angry at some point during the multiday clean-up, I
kicked one, which was already torn, and some papers
flew out, skipping and somersaulting across the yard
in the wind. I ran them down. One paper was the
pink middle copy of an official triplicate form. It was
a restraining order filled out by the wife against the
husband for "verbal and physical abuse." Another
form was a court summons, on which, in handwriting
(I assume from a cop), was a description of the offense
by the husband: *Holding loaded gun up in threatening
manner toward spouse and children.*

It was then, rummaging through the filth and what
felt like the ruin of my house, *my* house—that phrase
was absolutely ringing in my cranium by now—that
I became convinced the two bent gas pipes, each

causing a small and dangerous leak, which could have either poisoned everyone in the house or caused a conflagration, were murder attempts.

First I thought the wife was trying to kill the husband. Then I imagined the teenage son was trying to kill the husband, and that was why he was wearing a ski jacket in the house when I showed up that day—because he had just re-bent the pipe to set the deadly trap. Then I got to thinking the husband was clearly trying to kill the wife, teenage son, and new baby, but maybe he would have just shot them or beaten them to death since he didn't strike me as much of a planner, more of a frenzied, emotional killer. Finally I started to think it was maybe a murder-suicide setup by the wife or son, or the wife and son, an attempt to end the whole miserable family with a flick of a lighter or a stove ignition. A mystery in the end. But somebody was trying to kill somebody. Of that I'm convinced. In *my* house.

HALF OF WHAT
I THOUGHT I KNEW
(OR, CRIMINALS BEFORE
THEIR CRIMES)

I remember.

I threw the spelling bee. I was eleven, in sixth grade. My teacher was Mrs. C. She often said things like, *Matthew, please remove your finger from your nostril,* or *Greg, if you must scratch your crotch in class, perhaps it is because you do not bathe properly or frequently enough.* Her comments were clearly enunciated daggers, correct English fashioned into a weapon, meant to be both mellifluous and to inflict maximum harm. But I liked her, liked her passive-aggressive streak, her barbed repartee, the barely contained animus she had for children. I wasn't sure, even as a child, that children were all that likeable.

Mrs. C had a degree in English, about which she often reminded the class, standing in her trim red or green or navy business suit and heels at the front of the room. She had studied Shakespeare and Jane Austen, the Bible, and the Romantic poets. Her hair was short and frosted and perfectly coiffed, a hair-spray shiny globe under the industrial, fluorescent lights of American public education. A lover of language and literature, she valued a world completely foreign to me (at our house there was the *Good News Bible* and, beside the toilet, *Reader's Digest*, neither of which did I ever read). Her impractical skills—cultural, artistic, underappreciated—had washed her onto a desolate shore with thirty elementary schoolkids who had cowlicks and crust around their wandering eyes and problems with grammar, punctuation, and usage, never mind manners, behavior, and hygiene.

Roughly a third of my class came from "good homes,"
meaning middle- and upper-middle-class homes
with professional, college-educated parents who
monitored the well-being of their children, cared about
homework and attendance, and had a conventional
notion and expectation of future success. To this
group, the American ideal of upward mobility and
improving your station in life was not only attainable
but assumed, and it was this set of beliefs that made
them truly privileged. They knew they would never be
disenfranchised, had been inculcated from birth into
believing their cultural dominance was a birthright (I
mean, all the successful characters on TV looked and
dressed just like their parents!).

Another third of the class—I was here—were Southern,
working-class stock. We had parents who were world-
weary and smart in relation to the immediate needs of
their lives, but with no formal education beyond high
school, and often a skepticism bordering on animosity
toward anything intellectual or artistic. For them—for
us, that is—organized, public education was a job that
needed to be endured until you faced the hard and fast-
approaching truths of work and marriage. But they
were "good Christians," that common compliment of
my South, folks wanting to be seen as doing right, and
thus corrigible. Our God wasn't above striking down
sinners, or whole civilizations, for that matter. If you
kept your nose clean, though, you'd get your reward in
the next life, which made muddling through this one

something that wouldn't necessarily drive you insane. Philosophizing about any of this was simply the creation of new problems—"sixties crap," said my dad—and no good to anyone. My grandmother's phrase "hogwash" could instantly incinerate any complicated idea.

Finally, there was a last third from the poor side of our city—viewed by all as a lesser form of humanity. They lived near the swamps along the Back River of Tidewater, Virginia, a place of helixing mosquito clouds, chattering frogs, cobbled-together, heatless shacks, and rumors of inbreeding, abuse, and lawlessness, some of which were true.

I couldn't win the spelling bee, though Mrs. C expected me to. That's what I remember. There was a force—let's call it a cultural undercurrent—holding me back, and I've thought a lot about this for a couple of decades now, at least since grad school, when I first read Birmingham School cultural studies critics and British working-class writers like Richard Hoggart (*The Uses of Literacy)* and Raymond Williams (*The Country and the City*). They wrote about growing up in England and Wales, but their stories of feeling lost inside of their own educational upward mobility, their painful separations from the comforts and values of their pasts and families, felt like my story. Actually, it *was* my story.

Briefly, the scene: It's May, sunny. Light through the windows. End of the year sixth-grade spelling-bee qualifier, where the winner from each class will compete to be champ of the grade. There are three pupils left, standing in front of Mrs. C and the students, and they inhabit, precisely, the three tiers of the class strata I named above. There is a girl—let's call her Lucy—from the upper-middle class, and her parents are already angling for her to go to Duke or at least Davidson or William & Mary on an academic scholarship. There is me, a little nervous because I've come farther than I meant to, and my flunky friends are already sniggling in the back row because I'm a finalist in the spelling bee, which is so totally "gay"—the bigoted catchword for all things stupid and detestable. And there is Melvin, a bright kid from a poor and profoundly dysfunctional family with a couple of older brothers headed, shortly, to jail. The three of us are a representative snapshot of white America: the haves-and-will-have-mores; the potentially-upwardly-mobile-but-choices-will-matter; and the absolutely-screwed-barring-a-miracle.

Jump ahead. Lightning round, single elimination. My turn came. The word was "onomatopoeia," which I had spelled only a week before on a test. Mrs. C smiled, and in the smile was something beyond her just knowing I could spell the word with ease. The something, I think, was a vision of my future made better by her, for she was, despite all I have said, a caring and serious teacher—a good teacher, one any kid would be lucky to have. She knew, had resigned herself sadly to knowing, that Melvin, no matter what happened academically, would have obstacle upon obstacle stacked before him—no family stability, poverty, probably a taste of victimizing sex and the spectacle of unmediated, mind-freak violence before he was a teen (it's a point of fact that most violence happens in the bottom of the socio-economic scale, but we don't think of it as a class issue; it's another point of fact that over 90 percent of violence is perpetrated by men, but we don't consider it a gender issue). Mrs. C knew Lucy would most likely succeed because she was surrounded by success, learning, and a nurturing and challenging home. But me? I was on the fence. Some kids like the one I was, "at-risk" kids, from families with "challenges," ended up in jail; others became college-educated professionals—kindergarten teachers, warehouse managers, social services personnel, owners of their own small businesses. A world of belonging and "success" was not out of reach for me, Mrs. C knew; but a world of abject criminality and drugs, which was within arm's reach to me at all times, wasn't either. I had loving but busy parents, who wanted what was best for me without having the tools—

socially, economically, intellectually—to know, at least in an abstract way, what exactly that was (though it definitely needed to involve money), or where it could be gotten, or what it would entail. We knew, for instance, that Duke was good at basketball but had no idea what a social science like anthropology even was.

What happened was this: I purposefully mixed up the e and the o. I could say that my friends' sniggling in the back was like a shiny social gun against my temple, spurring me to bad decisions, bad things, but that would miss the much bigger question about how we learned our values and attitudes, why we thought of organized education as a joke. Melvin gave it a go, but he thought there was a D instead of a T (but hey, the kid had to do his homework on the floor in a dirty corner of a crowded, noisy house). Lucy nailed it, as expected, later winning the whole sixth grade. The three of us played our roles perfectly without knowing we had roles to play. If we thought about our identities at all, it certainly was not in relation to the broad, systematic forces shaping us, or how a shuffling of backgrounds would have most likely meant a flip-flopping of spelling-bee results.

As I left the class, Mrs. C's expression was one I'd never seen from her before. It was beaten, disappointed. "You know it's 'oeia'," she said. "You just spelled it correctly last week." I told her I forgot, was nervous. What I didn't tell her, what I couldn't have told her then or for a long time after, was that she did not function for me as an authority. My parents, who worked all the time—for they too wanted the prizes of American life, a bigger house, a couple of cars—were also no real authority anymore. Instead, I'd been partly raised by a television and by a demographically marketed and carefully produced faux–rock 'n' roll aesthetic, and by my friends, who had also been raised by a television and a demographically marketed and carefully produced faux–rock 'n' roll aesthetic, which had convinced us that real power and authority lay in an ahistorical idea of "cool," a cheap, commercialized version of rebellion with no context, no origin we could understand. We performed this rebellion without ideal, without understanding what might be legitimate to resist, which is a way of taking the darkest aspects of adolescent emotion and bending them toward cynicism, nihilism, a fatalistic and negative style with no substance, a laziness padded with delusion. My friends and I were—yes, the irony here is gargantuan—pitifully clueless conformists. That's C-O-N-F-O-R-M-I-S-T-S.

If I could find Mrs. C. now, I'd try to explain that moment in the classroom, how we imagined ourselves to be something we were not, in our mixed-up little media minds. I'd tell her that some of those friends of mine in the back row ended up with arrest records or dead. A lot of them, actually. And I'd tell her I've had to work hard, think hard, to unlearn about half of what I thought I knew.

TWO BODIES

Finding the second body was worse. How could it not have been, even though the first one was a white kid and the second was a black kid, a poor black kid, and truth be told he had a lot of issues with all the damn food-stamp blacks who had moved into the new projects the city built so close to his neighborhood during the time he was away. Still, the black kid in 2005—*that* body—was only four years old. The white kid, all those years before, in 1983, had been thirteen. Don't get him wrong, the white kid was bad, *nightmare* bad, cramped-stomach, ringing-in-the-ears, daytime-spooky-visions bad, but not *as* bad. A tiny four-year-old child like that, a disfigured, tortured corpse—it does something to your mind. You see it and then life gets split into before the seeing and after the seeing.

And who finds *two* bodies in the woods behind his house,

he wanted to know. Hampton, Virginia, has plenty of crime, sure—drug violence, poor people daily wrecking other poor people—but it's not exactly Sarajevo or Cape Town or Chicago. *Two bodies.* Two dead kids a football-field distance from where he laid his head.

The first body, the thirteen-year-old, was a Boy

Scout. He had walked to a friend's home through the woods that were sandwiched between the two friends' neighborhoods. He didn't come home for dinner. His mother called the friend's house. Her son had never shown up, which was weird, very unlike him. Panic, but controlled. She called other friends. Nothing. Panic, less controlled. She called the cops. Wait twenty-four hours, they said. These things usually resolve themselves. Kids will be kids, you know, and boys especially. Her son was an A student, a Boy Scout, and—literally—a choir boy. By midnight full-scale panic.

Next morning it was clear the kid was *gone* gone. Everyone, even the cops, knew this, knew it wasn't a runaway situation, though they wanted to be methodical and keep the family calm. A kid like this gone often means a body will be found or, maybe worse, he is being "kept" for some perp's deranged fantasies. A search party was organized by the police, the kid's father, and neighbors. Flyers were printed. TV and newspaper coverage that morning.

This guy, the one who would later find the *other* body, went out with a group into the woods just behind the neighborhood. He was nineteen in 1983. He went with the group of men and boys who were to scour the nearest woods intentionally because he thought that would be the least likely place to actually find anything other than footprints maybe, or trash, possibly a candy wrapper the kid had dropped. He figured there was near zero chance of finding the Boy Scout.

A couple of cops, one man and one woman, instructed his group on how to fan out about twenty yards apart, to then move in a line forward, like a wave washing up on shore, eyes aiming at a thirty-degree angle ahead and sweeping left to right as they progressed.

Later, he would think it was almost ridiculous, like a bad dream. He had wanted to help, but when he walked up on the body, covered up with sticks and pine straw, he had a hard time believing his own eyes. His first thought was that someone was playing a macabre joke on him, burying a blow-up doll or a mannequin where he would find it. Dead bodies have a rubber look to them. Years later, he probably thought about that a lot, how dead bodies don't look like living bodies, how something very fundamental happens to this shell we're in when we pass from alive to dead.

The dead boy, the first dead boy, was a kid I knew. He

had been raped and strangled with his own sock. DNA evidence strewn around like confetti. I lived in this neighborhood until 1977. I didn't know the body finder, who was seven years older than me and whose house was a couple of blocks away from my own. I found out about him many years later, after my schizophrenic brother falsely admitted to this murder, admitted to raping and murdering a thirteen-year-old Boy Scout.

So: Our body finder, our *double* body finder, walked up

on the first corpse. A total horror show, but the thing is, you get over stuff, you do, you forget it or repress it in a way that helps your world to keep spinning. (I think Freud really screwed things up for repression.) You get up the next day and the first thing you think about is the lifeless body. Sure. But then six months later you can go a few days without it entering your mind. After a while, eighteen months, say, or two years, he didn't think of it much, not until he found the second body in 2005. Then he couldn't get *either* body out of his head. He lost a lot of sleep after that second one. He thought maybe he had PTSD, caught it like a cold.

He had been gone for twenty years between the times

the bodies were dumped in the woods. Went out west, to the Rockies. Tried a little college but that didn't work out. Not really a book guy. He got married and had two kids, two boys. Messy divorce. New girlfriend. His parents went to a retirement community and he could move into their house in the old neighborhood. Money tight, he saw this as the way out of struggle and debt. Go back to Hampton, to the old house, a little brick rancher on a black-topped street of similar houses, my old house just two blocks down the road.

The second kid's name was Devon. Four years old, like

I said. He lived with his aunt because his mother was
a crackhead and she had been going out for half a day,
a day, getting high and leaving the kid at home by
himself. She'd come back to the apartment and find him
with a lamp knocked over, or his arm stuck behind a hot
radiator, and she was barely out of her teens anyway
and understood how to care for or even care about a
child about as well as she understood the mating habits
of Galapagos lizards. She couldn't get why he wouldn't
just *understand* her instructions the way, say, a ten- or
twelve-year-old would have, so she'd come home bug-
eyed and vaporized, her fellow-feeling shrink-wrapped
and on ice, and beat him, punch him in the back, in the
kidneys, slam his head against the wall. She couldn't
take the crying. And she hated the boy's father. No-
count motherfucking drug addict.

Devon's grandmother took him away to her apartment.
Last thing she needed was social services coming
around and fucking with her daughter's situation and
getting them all up in court waiting around all damn
day for some judge or social worker to say this or that
and end up costing them money. Grandma was only
about forty and she liked to party herself. Devon staying
with her didn't work out because she never signed up for
a little boy walking around and she had her own life. So
then Devon's aunt took him—she was the responsible
one; but responsible is relative, of course, and she
was poor and had to work and she'd leave the kid for
hours by himself as well, had to. Sometimes she'd ask
a neighbor from one of the other apartments to check

in on him, but she didn't trust most of her neighbors, whom she thought would have checked on the kid and then stolen some of her utensils or earrings or a pair of shoes or something.

Devon's aunt's boyfriend moved in. He didn't have a job so he stayed with the kid. He was the one who called the police to say that he stepped out of the house for just a minute to go to the mart to get some cigs, got caught up with some friends and maybe had a drink or two, and came back and Devon was gone. Disappeared.
There is a lot of poverty in Hampton, Virginia, the

city where I was born, plenty of white poverty, sure, but a tsunami of black poverty, whole neighborhoods and apartment complexes filled with human beings written off by their society. But credit to the police for showing real care about the Devon case. Flyers went out immediately. Nightly news coverage. A plea for any information from a police spokesman. Search parties. A helicopter!

This is just my opinion, my reading of our culture and history, my thoughts on race in America, and especially in Southern cities with moderate to high crime rates, like the one I am from, but I don't think quite the same force and focus would have been marshaled for a little black kid back in 1983, when the white Boy Scout I knew went missing. The fact that black professionals had moved into many positions of power within the city in the interceding twenty-two years (the twenty years white people, including my family, were moving out of the city) had erased some of the centuries-long double standard for how to deal with missing white kids and missing poor black kids. They did their best for Devon. Here is what the body finder told the paper after

Devon's body was discovered within a hundred feet of where he came across the first body: He talked about how people were passing out fliers with Devon's picture and a number to call. He talked about his feeling of déjà vu and how he was gone for twenty years, and now he had two children and came back and for this to happen—crazy. He talked about how strange it is when stories go from the TV screen right to your neighborhood. He said it makes you think about a lot of stuff. He said he kind of felt like a character on TV answering questions, an act which would later be on TV. Then he shook his head and said: No further comment.

This isn't an episode of *CSI*. It's a story, sure, but I've decided to jettison most of the confected nature of short fiction for this book. Criminals are almost never masterminds, and more often than not they are impulsive and profoundly stupid. The most obvious culprit is usually the culprit. There is evil in the world, and I mean a force that can and does run easily through all of us, but I think what is more dangerous is how we have widespread social circumstances, a breeding ground if you will, that create a system of values that is inhuman, cold, and predicated on a disregard for life, which can become a fast conduit for what is worst in us. Chris Hedges: "Once communities break down physically, they break down morally." It's the reason we've relied on religion, government, and laws since the first handful of people sat together around a campfire. Each of these institutions and systems at base has this to say to us: *No matter how bad things get, please don't fucking kill each other.*

Devon's injuries included liver damage from repeated blows, multiple burns on his arms and legs (which had been bandaged with duct tape), deep fingernail marks, and at least thirteen separate wounds on his head from a blunt object such as a pan. What killed him, however, was a snapped neck, most likely caused by someone putting a knee in his back and pulling the head back with extreme force.

The aunt's boyfriend, the "babysitter," had latex gloves in his kitchen. He also had seven empty bottles of bleach and a cooler full of bleach, which he had used to clean the house. The boy's blood was still found in the house, despite the cleaning. The boyfriend was charged with the murder of the child. The aunt and mother were both charged with child abuse and neglect and perjury. All three went to jail, the boyfriend possibly for the rest of his life.

The body finder wasn't one of the first ones on the scene

for Devon, as he had been with the Boy Scout, so maybe
technically he didn't *find* both bodies—only the first. But
he walked up as the cops and several searchers were
yellow-taping off the site to wait for the crime scene
techs. He saw the body, just a little kid, covered in dirt
and filth and pine straw, lifeless, and it messed with his
mind for a while, bringing up images of both bodies.

He still lives in that neighborhood, my old neighborhood,
in his parents' brick rancher. After the second body, his
boys were not allowed to go into the woods behind the
house, which took on, in his mind, a dark and mythic
power, like a place in a fairy tale that swallows children.

Some years ago I drove the streets of my old neighborhood.

I was writing a different book, and sometimes when I'm writing a book, fiction or nonfiction or some kind of mix like this one, I like to spend a lot of time on set, if you will, looking around, listening. I parked and got out of my car. I walked the sidewalks. Everything was quiet. A peaceful neighborhood, if a little run-down. I walked into the woods, along the paths near where the two bodies were found. I'd spent days out there as a little boy, which made this visit feel like entering some secret chamber of memory, of dream. The light, the smell, the trees, those vines—this was my life, my past!

I spent a couple of hours out there. Leaves, stumps,

rotting logs, spiderwebs so fine they looked like fog from a distance. In the midst of densely populated suburbs, I saw squirrels, robins, blue jays, and even a yellow-eyed owl whose head swiveled and eyes tracked me as I walked. There was a carpet of brown pine needles on the ground, their gin scent pungent in the air. The earth there is flat, like a wood floor, and the trees are wide apart, and as I stood, morning sun slanted through those trees, which were black against the crashing bright light, the whole tableau briefly like a stained-glass mosaic. I tried to imagine the mind of the man I had read about in the paper, the man who had come across both bodies so close to his home. If he were to venture back into the woods, I thought, walk around as I was doing, even right in the area where the murdered boys were found, he would have to realize that you can't blame nature for the horrors people do.

EASY ROLLER

The breaking and entering could have been avoided.
That was stupid. But he was drinking back then,
drinking a lot, four or five or six shots of bourbon,
almost always bourbon, *before* he went out to the city
bars to start what he considered the proper, the *real*,
drinking. He wasn't thinking straight. "Three sheets
to the wind," he says, quoting his dead father's favorite
saying for someone drunk beyond sense, beyond humor,
beyond functioning. "Three sheets to the wind."

Nowadays, when he talks about this, about what
happened, how he feels he was forced to do what he
did to save himself, he spins it into a real crime drama,
all starting with this breaking and entering. So that's
where I'll start.

He was twenty-four. Middle-class kid. Loving parents.
Had attended a good public high school. He then
"attended" college, he often jokes, using finger quotation
marks, meaning: He went with friends to college parties;
he once or twice ate in a college dining hall; he owned
a sweatshirt with the college's name arced across the
chest, which was both a costume and business attire.

His proximity to the college was important. Colleges
are customer bases, hallowed halls of eager consumers.
Learn stuff, sure. Get high, definitely. And the college
was in a large Southern city, so this magnified the
potential for sales. Customers begetting customers.
His pot, for a while, was like a popular brand. His pot,
he says, was like Nike, or Tommy Hilfiger, or Samuel
Adams. "Yo, dank bud," is how he describes it. I imagine
a little copyright symbol beside that saying. Economics
101: Drugs and Capitalism. Final project: Dank bud.

He was coming home from a college party when it happened. It was two in the morning. He was driving the Mercedes he had purchased a few years earlier, using money he inherited when his father passed away in his mid-fifties after a grueling and dehumanizing two-year battle with stomach cancer. The car was white with chrome rims and gangsta-chic, just the way he wanted it, but it only cost a couple thousand bucks since it had been confiscated in a drug bust a year or so before he bought it at a police auction.

He was crocked on this night, both drunk and high. He noticed the cop car behind him as he drove through his neighborhood of small, working-class bungalows. He played it cool, though, no swerving, no erratic speeding and slowing, no suspicious brake-light winking, which he knew cued the cops to a late-night driver's nervousness.

After he pulled into his driveway, the cop car stopped, or at least slowed down—he can't exactly remember—and he sat frozen for a moment in the car in the cracked and grass-tufted driveway of his rental house, which his mother still helped him pay for. She didn't know about the pot, so he had to feign as if he were barely making it financially; he told her he was going to sign up for some continuing education classes through the university, which he wasn't going to do; he told her he was working part-time with a house-painter friend, a money-under-the-table kind of thing, which was a lie.

He had a lot to be nervous about as he sat in the dark car. Eighty things, to be precise, because in a back bedroom he had taped thick cardboard over the windows and set up an elaborate hydroponic growing system— timed misters, electricity-gorging rows of mail-ordered lights, two carefully set heaters on either side of the room. He had, on the night the cop followed him and then stopped, or at least slowed down, eighty mature pot plants very close to being harvested for sale to all those college customers.

Once the cop had motored by, he went into the house through the back door, locking the door handle behind him. He clicked on the lights and paced around the kitchen. Then he clicked off the lights so no one could see into the house. He went to the front window and pulled the curtain back a few inches and peered out at the driveway. No one around. The only light was from the two nearby streetlamps, which dropped in overlapping white baby pools onto the street. The rest of the neighborhood was as black as night sky.

He remembered, suddenly, he had left a roach, the burnt end of a joint, poking out of his ashtray. Panic tore through him. He feared the cop would come back, shine a light around in his car. Probable cause, big time. The inside of his house smelled like bong resin. Shit shit shit.

He hurried out into the dark to get the joint. But he was drunk and high, as I said, not thinking clearly, and when he got to his Merc—that's what he called it, the Merc—he realized he had left his keys in the kitchen. Car headlights swept slowly around the corner. He knew it was the cop again, and now he was convinced someone had ratted him out and the law was casing him and his house. They knew he was a dealer!

He ran back to the rear of the house. But he'd closed the back door, which turned and opened while locked from the inside but not, obviously, from the outside. A drunk's avoidable mistake. The cop, seeing some frenzied motion in the dark, had pulled into his driveway. Red and blue lights went on. He heard one *whuip* from the siren, then the inscrutable crackle of the cop's radio.

He needed to think, but he didn't have time, and his synapses weren't exactly at full strength, so he didn't think and did something that in hindsight was the real start of his downfall. He smashed through the backdoor window with his fist, which took three hard punches, then reached in and unlocked the door and let himself in. By then the cop was in the backyard, right outside the door, his gun drawn, flashlight in the other hand, telling him to put his hands up, put his hands up, put his hands up.

The door was wide open. He stood in the kitchen. The cop came into the house, crunching over the glass, which he could legally do now because of the break-in, the break-in to *his own house*, and all the ridiculously suspicious activity at two in the morning in a quiet suburban neighborhood. Because there was a gun and a light in his face, it wasn't until he put his hands up that he realized he had cut his wrist. A long gash went from his palm to about a quarter of the way up his arm, missing his main artery by millimeters. Blood drops the size of golf balls slapped the linoleum floor.

He stood in a crowded cell. There were ten, maybe twelve prisoners in the fifteen-by-fifteen-foot room, and all but he and one other tattooed, bald guy were black or Hispanic. He had been stitched up at the emergency room, two uniformed officers guarding him as a resident did the needlework. They had handcuffed his uncut arm to the rail of a hospital bed. He started off petulant, still drunk at that point, then began to weep like an eight-year-old. The cops thought he might not get through the medical procedure without sobering up first and then taking a heavy sedative for pain. Kid was a major wuss. White boys. *Jesus H!* The cops already knew he was going to roll.

After eighteen hours in jail, cramped with all the other prisoners, a cop came along and let him out and took him to a back room, an interview room. Concrete. Gray paint. Small, plain table and four orange, plastic chairs. Even what looked like a two-way mirror. It reminded him of *Homicide* or *The Wire*. The place had the feel of highly authentic gritty realism, which made sense, he figured, since it was in fact authentic gritty realism.

He had called his mom in tears. He had called his sister in tears. But he was in deep and they couldn't really help him beyond trying to find him an affordable lawyer, which would take at least a couple of days. Eighty pot plants, baggies, scales, all kinds of pot smoking paraphernalia around the house—there was clear intent to distribute.

The cop sat down. Then another cop came in, the one from the house. Middle-aged guys, a little chubby, both with crew cuts, one in a suit and the one who arrested him in a blue uniform. Really uncannily like *Homicide* or *The Wire*. First thing the suited cop from the narcotics division said was that he was facing fifteen to twenty years for the manufacture and distribution of narcotics. Going down. Requisite talk of the threat of rape in prison. Mention of all the really big, mean black guys from the projects locked up with him. Oh, Christ. More tears.

They put the wire in his pubic hair, just above
his genitals. It looked like the chopped-off top of
a microphone, but it was only about the size of a
quarter. That way if someone frisked him they'd likely
miss it, or he could play the homophobia card, say
watch my junk, etc.

It had taken him, oh, four or five minutes of threats
from the two cops to agree to rolling over on a bigger
drug connection. And he had an alcohol problem, so
while he was in jail for three days, he'd gotten the hum
and jitters like an old refrigerator, and wave after wave
of anxiety attacked him to the point that he thought he
was having a heart attack. The other prisoners started
calling him "stinky" or "stinky white boy" or "stinky ass
white motherfucker" or "stinky ass white motherfucking
bitch" because he was dropping onto the one filthy
toilet sticking out of the wall of the cell every half hour.
The commode was stainless steel and resembled a big-
butt-sized bedpan. His insides sounded like someone in
boots stomping around in thick mud. He knew he'd kill
himself if he was sentenced to a penitentiary. He said
he'd hang himself; he'd slit his own throat. I doubt he
had the nerve to do either.

It wasn't all rash thinking, though. He did consider whom to roll on fairly carefully. It needed to be a serious player, a distributor of pot, coke, or maybe even heroin. It needed to be someone who'd definitely have way more drugs than he had, or he'd end up going down anyway. It needed to be someone who wouldn't, or probably wouldn't, or at least *maybe* wouldn't, send someone to kill him.

He knew this guy, the brother of a friend, a family man with a wife—or maybe she was a girlfriend—and two little kids. He was a holder, meaning that he would store for a time a dealer's hard drugs, mostly vacuum-packed bricks of heroin. The serious dealers were all on the radar of the city cops. So this guy, who lived in a nice suburban house and looked like an accountant or bank manager, would "hold" bulk for them until right before a deal went down. Then he'd get a nice kickback. Had worked for years, and he owned a nice house, a minivan, and a new Honda Civic to show for it. His kids went to a good school, did summer camps. Neighborhood cookouts were held in his backyard, just yards away from vacuum-packed bricks of hidden powder soon to be in some junky's veins.

They met in a Starbuck's.

What's up? asked the holder, once they sat down with their coffees.

I was hoping to get Jay's number from you, he said. I've got something he might be interested in. Didn't want to talk on the phone, right.

The wire was itching his crotch. He had armpit sweat stains the size of softballs. His forehead looked like a rain-crossed windshield in Seattle.

The holder looked at him. Then said: I don't know anyone by that name.

Look, man, he said. I know you've got his horse at your house. I know how much he sells. I just want to make contact. I've got something for him. A venture. Believe me, he'll be interested.

Like I said, said the holder, I have no idea who or what you're talking about.

Come on, man, he said. What you think, I'm a narc or something?

The holder looked at him. Then looked around the Starbuck's. Not exactly criminal digs. And it was what he said next that sunk him: Okay, I'll talk to Jay for you, and he can contact you if he wants. But I'm not giving you his number. And don't be such an idiot to talk about the shit in my house in a public place. Jesus, man. What is wrong with you? Use your fucking brain, man.

With no fanfare, two plain-clothes detectives picked up the holder in the parking lot, taking his latte out of his hand and putting him in the back of an unmarked police car.

He doesn't know what happened to the holder. This sort of thing is a sacrifice. You do it and you don't look back. The cops said thanks and let him go with no charges— after, of course, they confiscated all of his drugs and growing equipment. He figures the holder rolled, too, rolled on someone really high up in the trade. What else can you do?

He does think sometimes about ruining the guy's life, destroying his family. But he couldn't do jail. Fifteen to twenty years? No way. Someone had to go down for his stupidity and damned if it would be him.

He moved into a small cottage out in the country after all this went down. His mom picked up the rent until he could figure something out. He told her he had clinical depression and couldn't work, not now.

About two months after he had worn the wire, just before he moved to the cottage, some young punks he'd never seen before in a tricked-out Subaru had started driving by his house ten or twelve times a day. Once they pulled into his driveway and just sat there, eating Burger King, then threw all their trash in his yard and left. It scared him so badly he packed up his minimal belongings, crammed them into a small U-Haul (paid for, again, by his loving, enabling mom), and moved out on a Saturday afternoon with two months left on his lease. Just abandoned his house.

No one has found him yet out in the country, at least
not that he knows of. His mom still helps with the
rent, but he's out working odd jobs now. He has two
dogs and two handguns. Hasn't had a drink in a year.
He takes Xanax and Paxil. When he isn't working,
which is a lot, he watches TV and plays Xbox all day
with the shades drawn. He's put on forty pounds. He
wears nothing but sweat suits or gym shorts because
none of his other clothes fit. He blames the weight
gain on the antidepressants. His sleep patterns are
screwed. Nowadays, every time he leaves the house—
to go to the grocery store or the post office or to the
drive-through at the McDonald's in the next town
over—he feels like there's a target on the back of his
head. He's keeping a lookout for that tricked-out
Subaru. He still says he had to do what he did.

A COUPLE OF WAYS
TO KILL YOURSELF

The last time I saw him was at an ATM machine. I was visiting the city where I grew up. What year was this?

He turned from getting his cash, saw me, hesitated. He said, What's up, dog?

Here is how we used to talk.

I was a little slow, unsure. That feeling of seeing someone you don't want to see, a ghost from the past. The sun was blazing. My face felt hot. Sweat dripped down my back, sticking shirt to skin.

Not much, man, I said, which is how I used to talk when I knew him as a teenager, but is not how I talk now. I repeated, for lack of anything else to say, Not much, man. We shook hands.

I hadn't seen him in five, maybe six years, since we were both in our mid-twenties, and then only briefly, long enough to say hello at a mall during the winter holidays. But I'd heard the stories, like a lot of people around here. He knew I'd heard the stories, which was why, I assumed, he'd hesitated—to gauge me, see from my face if I was judging.

That's part of this type of awkward exchange—a trope of American working-class life—between the person who left, who "made something of himself" (it's never so simple), and the person who stayed not by choice but because he created a life with no other options. He had been wracked by addictions, inertia, and a series of bad decisions (dropped out of trade school, didn't wear condoms) and small tragedies of his own making (crashed cars, drug charges and jail time, bones broken during drunken roughhousing). He is—he was—an example of some of the boys and men with whom I grew up, ones who get into a fist fight with a cousin's friend at his brother-in-law's Sunday barbecue, the cops showing up, the neighbors lining the sidewalks, shaking their heads, the two fighters spitting-mad and red-faced and in torn shirts or shirtless in the driveway, doing a reality-television-show dance of "hold-me-back, hold-me-back."

He was big, 6' 3" or 6' 4", towering over me as we unclasped hands. He had long blond hair and a scraggly goatee; broad shoulders, a pot belly and a bloated face from too much, probably *way* too much, drinking. He wore a Corona T-shirt, army-green cargo shorts, and flip-flops. I remember thinking about how big his feet were, the size of a child's swim flippers, and he was pigeon-toed, right foot aiming southwest, left foot southeast.

I smiled—at the feet, but he didn't know that—killing some tension.

He asked where the hell I'd been, where I lived, what I

did. I left at seventeen for college and have only been a visitor since. I told him I lived in New England, not far from the Canadian border. I was a professor.

Go *on*, he said. Are you messing with me? A southern boy up there in the damn Arctic. And what would they let you be a professor of?

Here was a bit of our old banter, which was always half a step from insult, two or three steps from face punch. I took no offense. I mean, he was right. He knew me as an adolescent and teen. The kids I hung around stole things, took drugs, drank like seasoned, middle-aged alcoholics. What would someone make me a professor of? Rail-grinding your skateboard? Telling dirty jokes? Jimmying a door lock?

I told him I was a creative writing professor.

He laughed, really guffawed, said: They teach rich kids to be creative?

And then I saw there was a kid with him, a little boy, maybe six, now sticking his buzz-cut head out of the window of the compact car parked along the sidewalk of the bank. Daddy, said the boy. Daddy.

The skin around the boy's left eye was purple-blue, one cherry-red horizontal line just below his lower eyelashes. I remember thinking, *he beat his kid*, though I had no way of knowing this and no reason to assume it. But I remembered his temper, his right hook, his left cross. I remembered him spitting in a girl's hair once, remembered seeing him beat a drunken kid up at a party for the hell of it, the fun of it, and then piss on him. I think it was those last acts of pure, gleeful meanness—not just touching the edge of menace anymore—that drove me away from him, made me feel if I didn't get away I was holding hands with the devil, I was spitting on girls and pissing on drunken kids, and no matter how bad I was—and I was on the periphery of some bad stuff for a while—I didn't want to go around hurting people. It became his hobby.

Hold on, boy, he said sharply without turning his gaze from me. Get back in your seat.

Daddy.

Get back in your seat!

But, Daddy...

Boy...

His son got back in his seat. I knew my old friend had been in a brawl at a bowling alley with a famous basketball star and the star's "posse" of friends over some back-and-forth racial epithets. I had seen articles about it in the newspaper—it made the national news and set off near-riots in the already racially uneasy place where I grew up (where the first African slaves were brought to America in 1619)—the focus of which was star athletes and legal troubles. But there was my old friend, this guy before me, mentioned by name several times and called the probable "instigator" of the incident. It also mentioned his short, drug-related arrest record.

Likes to talk, that boy, he said, pointing a thumb at the car, smiling. Like his mom, my old girlfriend, yak yak yak, you know.

He spit a thick glob right into the middle of the walkway in front of the cash machine, everything still his to deface.

I also knew he had been strung out on cocaine (and I'm fairly sure crack) and heroin for years, with a few unsuccessful attempts at rehab. Curious, I've always thought, how some kids can smoke a first joint or have a first drink and continue on in life without being destroyed; others—is it chemical makeup, psychological predisposition?—almost immediately after a first encounter with narcotics and alcohol, aim their lives toward addiction, disconnection from self and others, squalor, and despair. They crave drugs daily, at any cost, at all cost, like basic nourishment. A pitiful, broken egotism takes hold. Reality warps. Relationships crumble. Bad karma haunts all things. I knew he was estranged from his mother and father, who were well-meaning and loving parents, a tradesman and a maid, estranged from his brother, who had gone to work with their father as a plumber and become a churchgoing dad and husband, a Neighborhood Watch organizer, a T-ball coach.

Daaaaady! the boy called, crying now.

My old friend turned. What? he said sharply in the direction of the idling car.

I couldn't hold it I couldn't hold it I couldn't hold it sorry sorry sorry. The child was hysterical, wailing, panicked.

My old friend walked with determined speed back to the passenger side of the car, opened the door, threw the front bucket seat forward, and poked his head and upper body into the backseat. I thought he would hit the child. He grabbed the crying boy's arm and said something I couldn't hear, which sent the boy's crying up a decibel. He then got out of the car, slammed the passenger-side door, and flashed me a cursory, petulant wave. He said nothing. He walked to the driver's side, got in, and drove out of the parking lot at twice a reasonable speed.

Here, I assume, is why I remember this: Many years later, I heard another story about him. His six-year-old was an adolescent by then. My old friend and his last girlfriend, a bar waitress, had been up for going on two days straight, drinking and doing speedballs (an injected mixture of cocaine and heroin). There was a fight. She ripped his clothes and locked him out of his rental house. He banged on the door, threatened her. Police came. But he and his girlfriend apologized, said everything was okay, no one was going to press charges, just a misunderstanding, sorry. When the cops left they went back inside, made up, and did more drugs. He passed out, looked a little blue in the face. She decided to go to sleep beside him and check on him in the morning. What could happen?

He was thirty-five years old, dead of what was later simply called a "heart attack."

When I started writing this story, my intention was to remember the scene at the ATM (what a perfect American setting!) and somehow—I didn't know how, I never do when I sit down to write—bend meaning toward compassion for my old friend in all his carelessness and pathetic threat. I wanted to figure out a rationale for his behavior, its complex cultural causes having to do with apathy, selfishness, provincialism, and the darker codes of masculine performance, trying to convince readers that they, too, should conjure sympathy for such a crooked, broken soul.

But it's not going to work, I see now. Meaning has morphed in the telling. Nothing here engenders sympathy for him. I don't *feel* sympathy, for him or for the kid I was when I knew him.

Truth is, when I heard he had died, I remembered him spitting on the girl, and beating up and pissing on the drunken kid, and pushing his parents, decent and loving people, to the edge of nervous breakdown, destroying their peace and happiness. I remembered especially his son's black eye, and the shrill fear in the child's screaming in the parking lot, screaming that said he knew what was coming.

My old friend and a previous version of me were
once nearly inseparable, and alike in many ways,
two kids among many headed for trouble, for bitter
dysfunction, early death, or jail time. To be honest, to
be totally honest—which we should do every once in a
while—I'm glad we're dead.

RABBIT DOG GUN

This shooting took place in the backyard of a suburban home. It was a planned community—every house one of four vinyl-sided, two-storey models and colors; well-tended flower beds in the street medians and along the sidewalks; elderly crossing guards at every corner when the kids got out of school—so the four reports—*crack, crack, crack, crack*—resulted in several neighbors calling the police.

The shooter was a friend of mine, a good friend for a time, and he must have been fifteen or sixteen when the shooting occurred. I was a different version of myself back then, as I've already said, something of a stranger and a mystery to the self I am now, the one doing the talking, the writing. I think his edginess was the attraction for me. I *think*. But time erodes absolute veracity. Memory bends to the will of our present selves' understandings and emotional needs. What happened: past tense is always a kind of fiction. But he had this volatility—he cursed at umpires during Little League games, he threw his helmet when something went wrong during football practice. His competitive nature and his temper were legendary. But he was a cool jock in that very classic, even archetypal, American way—good-looking, popular, a versatile athlete, one of the best players on any team, in any activity. We had played several sports together. Drifted around in the same circles. We were friends without really knowing a damn thing about each other. Sports friends. High school friends. Close strangers.

The black and white, long-haired rabbit was his sister's. It lived in a wire pen in the backyard. His sister was older than we were, maybe twenty, and she had a first baby from a boyfriend who was long-gone by the time this happened (she later had four more kids with four different men, one of whom she met in a waiting room while about to pick up her second or third husband from a Narcotics Anonymous meeting). The rabbit was almost catatonically fat, I remember, but it was the baby's pet, or would be the baby's pet when the baby was a toddler and then a preschooler and old enough to know what a pet was. The family had attached a lot of value to this unmoving rabbit—because of the baby.

So I'm over there after school one day. Fall, I think.
Sunny, brisk. Let's say 1986. Could have been 1987.
The sister screams from the backyard. Through the
sliding-glass door we can see her with the baby on her
hip. Three or four sports dudes are sitting around the
kitchen table eating Pop-Tarts and cereal after school (I
tended to drift back and forth between the skater/surfer
kids of Tidewater and the organized-sports jocks, since I
loved, and still love, athletics). My friend's mom and dad
are at work until six. Kitchen full of big, testosterone-
filled boys. B.O. and farts and cursing and sex jokes.

My friend jumps up from the table, opens the sliding
glass door. He runs. The rest of us funnel out behind
him, having no idea what's going on.

In the rabbit pen is a dachshund, brown with a black
nose, big, floppy ears. It's stuck inside after somehow
burrowing its way in to get to the rabbit. The rabbit is a
bloody hunk of hair, lifeless as a stuffed toy.

A bad scene all around. Dead rabbit, cowering dog now
locked in the pen. A screaming and crying and already
pretty fucked-up and unhinged twenty-year-old with
a baby on her hip. Caterwauling child. Three or four
pumped-up jocks standing around saying, "Damn, man"
and "Sheeeeiiiit" and "No way." Tragic ingredients, no?

What to do? What to do?

Someone suggested calling animal control. *Do they still,*

like, have dog catchers? Call the people whose dog it is. Yeah, there you go. Make them buy the baby a new rabbit.

As we were still discussing options, discussing the generally surreal nature of the whole situation in front of us, before anyone knew what was happening, before anyone even realized my old friend the bad-tempered athlete had gone inside and come back out again, he, my old friend, pointed his father's .22 pistol at the head of the whimpering brown dachshund and put four bullets through its neck and skull—*crack, crack, crack, crack.* He then screamed and kicked the pen and yelled "fuck fuck fuck" much as he did when things went badly at a football practice, only now he had a pistol in his hand and dog blood all over the grass near his feet.

I can see him now. But the thing is, I grew up in suburban America, right, I grew up on TV and movies, hours and hours, half a lifetime really, so my mind and memories, my *consciousness*, is a mediated thing, reality and fantasy blended into an "I," and I see this whole debacle as if it's all framed within a shot that could have played on one of those ABC after-school specials for latchkey wanderers like me. Lives, supposedly real lives, packed into fifty minutes, then equally divided by commercials for Spaghetti-O's or another TV show or for other products you didn't need. Sometimes when I remember this, I think maybe it never happened, that I dreamed it, or I really did just watch it on TV, and what I am remembering is just that, a strange and bad dream or a strange and bad melodrama I should go ahead and forget. But recently I made a few calls to people I knew back then. Interviews, I guess, though not very official. It did happen. And pretty much exactly the way I'm remembering it here.

The baby was crying. My friend's sister was now really in hysterics. All the rest of us possessed faces of disbelief, even mild shock. Did we just *see* that? Our friend murder a little yipper dog beside a dead, incisor-punctured bunny? Is this a David Lynch film?

I made a Bee-line for home, dazed and sick not just in my gut but in my soul, so I didn't see what happened after that.

The shooter's father was an engineer, a good guy by all accounts, if perhaps a little too busy to parent his half-unhinged children. He paid off the neighbor for the dog, and worked hard to explain to this neighbor the importance of the rabbit to the baby, etc. He got a lawyer for his son, my old friend, who was charged with cruelty to animals and discharging a firearm within 500 feet of several residential houses. He then put his one gun in a locked safe and hid the key from both his son and daughter, who were not, he fully understood, exactly upstanding or stable citizens. I'm sure he still had fond memories of the two of them when they were young and less sullied by cynicism and life, but I don't think he had a clue about what kinds of storms swept through their heads at that point. He went to work. They wandered around in their familiar and materially comfortable settings lost, like about half the population.

My old friend got forty hours of community service. I think he volunteered at the hospital. Maybe it was the fire station. I don't know. It's been a long time.

Recently, I've been thinking about this guy, doing some quick research through Google and newspaper archives, calling old acquaintances that might have information.

Here is what I found: He got married. But within a couple years his wife had left him and evidently filed a restraining order against him. He had a few girlfriends after that, but once they got a preview of that deadly temper of his, they left him. His drinking then went from heavy to Olympian.

The good news is that he hasn't killed anyone. He's had three DWI's, in two different states, which are felony charges. He cannot legally own a gun, and I don't think he is quite dumb enough or desperate enough to try to procure an illegal one, which, given his temper, makes the world a slightly safer place.

I don't know what became of his sister and all her kids.

HIT AND RUN

He walked into a Norfolk, Virginia, 7-Eleven with a
steak knife stolen from a local diner in his jacket pocket.
He had spent the previous two days high on crack, but
now he was broke and coming down and desperate, and
whereas fear was a factor earlier in the day, keeping
him from robbing a store or a passerby because he
didn't want to get caught and end up in jail again,
where there were no drugs, he was bottoming out at the
moment, deep in what his public defender would later
call "street-drug psychosis"—teeth grinding, panicked,
eyes jaundiced and dancing in his face, just flat-out
suffering—so sense and caution were in the past, were
history, and he was moving *forward* and on a mission
and bent crooked to get some cash *now*. If he wasn't
high within the hour, he was sure he was going to die.

This was an inner-city store, a few blocks from
downtown and the business district. Maybe fifteen or
twenty people were in the aisles, by the coffeepots,
getting Big Gulps of soda or Slurpees. People in and out
all day and night. New customers every few minutes.

At the counter, he cut in line and told the woman
working the cash register to empty the drawer or he was
going to shoot. He looked down at his jacket pocket, at the
object poking forward, which wasn't shaped like a gun
muzzle at all, but he thought it was more threatening
to do a holdup with a gun than a cheap, dull steak knife
so he went with that. He didn't want to have to pull the
weapon out and stab anyone, but he would if he had to.

The woman refused. Crazy stuff like this happens in the poor neighborhoods of Norfolk on a daily basis, so she chalked it up to some desperate drug fiend behavior and looked at the next customer and said, Is that all, sir?

Bitch was disrespecting him. Thought he ought to stab her in the heart. But he needed to get out of the store fast and this wasn't going well. He turned to the man getting ready to purchase his items. He pointed his jacket pocket at him and said, Give me your money or I'll shoot you in the gut with this here pistol.

The man thought about the threat for a second. Was this whack job for real? Then, feeling it wasn't worth the possibility of getting shot—a lot of stupid death in these inner-city neighborhoods—he handed over a twenty-dollar bill. Our culprit turned and ran, bursting out through the glass doors and into the rest of his morning, which also happened to be my morning.

Twenty dollars in his pocket, he jogged through an alley, down a street, up another street, then started lifting the driver-side door handle of every car he passed. Locked, locked, locked. He came to a large nineteen-eighty-something Oldsmobile station wagon—white with wood panels, I remember—sitting in front of the stoop of an apartment building. Unlocked, keys in it, running. He opened the door and started driving away as an old woman, who had been quickly dropping off her granddaughter at a sitter's, ran down the stoop steps yelling for him to stop. Stop. Hey, that's my car!

His plan was to drive over to the projects, abandon the car along the road, unharmed except for his lingering rancid smell, and go on foot to get the crack. He'd smoke it right there in the stairwell of the building, ten paces from where he purchased it. Who cared in a place like that? And he was dying. He was trying to save himself.

He sped through the streets in the large car, cutting across lanes, accelerating, braking, accelerating. The white Nissan in front of him slowed to make a right turn. He assumed he'd timed their turn correctly and would just miss them, the corner of their bumper inching out of the lane as he roared by. But there were large potholes in the road onto which they were turning; it was a new sports car; the people inside stopped.

He drove right through the back quarter panel at about thirty-five miles per hour, throwing the car into more than a three-hundred-and-sixty-degree spin, leaving it up on the sidewalk, wedged against the pole of a parking meter, the couple inside tossed around like clothes in a dryer.

His head had smashed hard into the windshield upon impact. So as he drove on, the front of the stolen Oldsmobile smashed in, the right front wheel at an odd angle to the ground, bumping and bumping, he had blood running from the several deep cuts in his face and across his forehead. He couldn't see through the spider-webbed glass. He rolled along as far as he could get from the accident. Then he jumped out of the ruined and still moving car (I either saw this in the rearview mirror or dreamed it later) and started running in an ungraceful, injured lope along the street as the vehicle crashed into a light post.

Within a couple of minutes, he heard sirens. Here he
was, jonesing for crack, blood all over his face, his coat,
his shirt, and his hands, a dull steak knife in one pocket,
a stolen twenty in the other, running down a sidewalk.

He was now in the Ghent section of the city, which is
higher income housing and shops. He stood out on these
sidewalks. He slowed down. He thought for a second. He
walked into a health-food grocery store. He picked up
a red shopping basket and began walking around as if
he was shopping for tofu or pomegranates or fair-trade
coffee.

Since he was obviously strung out, not to mention
covered in blood, which was falling in drips onto the
floor as he perused, the manager called the police. Our
perpetrator was picked up by several officers within a
few minutes without incident. Real crime stories rarely
end in Hollywood bonanzas of violence. They usually
end more like this one, with someone covered in blood
saying, Who? Me?

A car accident sounds like a bomb going off inside your own head. When he drove through the back of us, spinning the world fast into a circle, throwing the whole car loudly up onto a sidewalk in front of a Laundromat and a jewelry store, I felt mostly a sense of unreality, a dreamy split second that somehow resembled the first moment after a nap—blank of meaning, disoriented. An instant or an eon; all the time before you were born or one blink.

My wife and I were in our mid-twenties. I had been driving her new car, a white Nissan 240 SX, a quick little sports car she'd had for only a few days. She loves sports cars, and she had her first job out of graduate school and was now finally the owner of one (the only one she would ever have). She was telling me how to drive it—stop, slow down, watch out for that pothole. We were bickering about who knew how to drive a stick better. Then there was some construction on the street onto which I was turning. Just pull over, she said, exasperated.

That's when the bomb went off inside my head, when time went through some mysterious changes.

Somehow I was lying down on the sidewalk beside the car. My wife was still in the front passenger seat. I got up, wobbly on my feet, head throbbing, and asked her if she was okay through the half-open window, but then I felt like puking so sat back down to finish my thought from a lower level. People had rushed up. Someone was yelling for us to just sit tight, don't move, the ambulance was on the way.

Worried, I mustered strength and got up to check on my wife again. I was shaken up but okay, I concluded. My wife seemed fine—perturbed about the car, but fine. After a minute—breathe in, breathe out, time getting its basic shape back—I asked her to get out of the car so we could sit down together and wait for the cops and ambulance.

Okay, she said. But she didn't get out.

Then I asked her if she was really okay, and though she looked just fine, she said, What? What happened? Where are we?

We were in an accident.

Oh, God.

We're okay.

My car. You didn't wreck my car, did you?

Well, you're *in* the car. I'm asking you to get out now. Okay. Okay. I think maybe you hit your head.

Did we take the new car this morning?

You're *in* the car. Just rest. Actually, don't get out. Relax. I hear the siren.

Then I almost passed out, though there was nothing
wrong with me except for some kind of post-accident
adrenaline dump. My wife sat stoically, if incoherently,
in the front seat and stared forward and never complained,
though she had, we would soon find out, a serious
concussion. This says a lot about who we are as
people and our whole marriage. I rode with her in the
ambulance to the hospital. She was hurt. I wasn't. She
didn't complain. I did.

At some point during the six or so hours in the hospital, a cop came by to take a statement from us. He told us the story about the crackhead, the 7-Eleven holdup with a steak knife, the stolen car (which I now remembered seeing briefly in the rearview mirror, but again, this could have been some kind of trauma-induced daydream), his limping and bleeding into a fancy grocery and pretending to be shopping. (The chance that I would eventually turn this experience into a story was pretty close to 100 percent.)

I was glad the cop told us this, because my wife was already pissed at me for the car wreck. Even later, when I was giving her the it-wasn't-me-it-was-the-crackhead spiel, she gave me a look that said it was me *and* the crackhead. Maybe even me *more than* the crackhead. At the very least some kind of collusion of stupidity and carelessness among the two drivers.

My wife could only eat popsicles for almost two days. She was pale, a hint of greenish-blue about her skin. She vomited several times. A concussion's symptoms look a lot like a brutal case of the stomach flu.

At some point as she was settled on the couch, I asked her if she was starting to feel any better, if she needed anything.

Yeah.

What?

What?

What do you need? I'll get it for you.

I'm fine.

Okay.

What?

Are you alright? Do you want to lie down?

I'm fine. Do I have homework?

Homework? You're not in school anymore. You finished grad school. You have a job. You bought a sports car. We were in an accident.
I feel like I have homework. I feel like maybe I'm

forgetting something. And I have a bump on my head. I think I bumped into something.

Then she'd have a popsicle. Then I'd hold her. Then she'd vomit. Then I'd help her back to the couch where we'd have another circular non-conversation.

A couple of years later, living in another part of the state—in the farmhouse I've told you about—that sports car long gone, we received a letter from a Virginia prison. I thought it probably had to do with my brother. I immediately started to feel sick and anxious—not this again.

But it was a short note from the crackhead, who was now an ex-crackhead working on street signs in the prison for a minimal stipend. He said he was sorry for running into us that day. He had a lot of problems back then. He was working to get better. He had written us a personal check for fifteen dollars, in an effort to pay us back for the nearly totaled car and any medical bills.

My wife still didn't remember much about the crash. She didn't even remember that much about being concussed and confused and sick after the crash, our weird non-conversations. But as for me, I was glad the guy had sent that short letter and check, since I was pretty sure that in some part of her mind my wife still blamed me for ruining her first and only sports car.

A NEW TRIAL

In 1999, seven years after my paranoid schizophrenic brother admitted to the 1983 rape and murder of a thirteen-year-old Hampton, Virginia, boy that he did not commit, while he was serving a twenty-year sentence for another crime—that of attempting to kill my father, mother, and younger brother in a botched arson—he was back in court for a new trial about the boy's death.

This time he was not the alleged criminal. He was called, against his will and on enough antipsychotics to fell a bronco, as a defense witness for the accused. The accused was one Willie Butler, a black man in his forties from a drug- and crime-ridden part of Newport News with a long rap sheet that included, among other things, assault, robbery, and lewd and lascivious behavior. Butler was in the maximum-security prison *with* my brother and thus knew him or at least knew of him. He knew my brother was in the psych wing with all the other mumblers and bumblers and God-is-talking-to-me prisoners, twitching or near-comatose men who had committed crimes like, say, gouging out their mother's eyes, or throwing a person off a building because the Pope had told them to through a secret message in an infomercial, or having a showdown with police that ended in them dressed in gasoline and setting themselves on fire. Butler and his public defender thought maybe they could use my mentally and emotionally impaired brother and his earlier incoherent confession to get off this murder rap, which probably meant life without parole, possibly the death penalty.

I followed the trial in the papers and on the news because I no longer had contact with my dangerous brother, wasn't about to show up in the courtroom.

Things had been going well for me. I had finished graduate school. I was married to a woman who'd never met a violent criminal, at least that she knew of. We had bought and were renovating the century-old farmhouse in the beautiful, green mountains of central Virginia, 175 miles from where I grew up and where the trial was taking place. I had a book coming out (a memoir/biography about my brother), and people were already talking to me about foreign rights and film rights, about which I knew nothing. I had just left a nice gig as an arts and culture journalist and editor for a magazine, was working on and off as a book critic, and was getting ready to take my first position as a writing professor, which came with a decent salary *and* health insurance. All good. More, probably, than I could have reasonably expected from life, all things considered. Then I heard—I can't even remember how or from whom now—about this trial.

The new trial came about because of DNA technology. Unsolved murder cases with logged evidence such as blood, hair, or semen were ever so slowly being run through the computer system up against the DNA of current Virginia prisoners. The collected semen from the 1983 case of the raped and murdered Boy Scout, which happened in the woods behind the neighborhood where I lived as a kid, came up as Willie Butler's, who had been out of prison for only a few weeks when the murder occurred and was back in for an unrelated crime shortly after. He was never a suspect.

In 1992, believing he could absolve the world of sin by absorbing all sin into himself, à la Jesus, my brother, who was twenty-five, hopped the fence of a psychiatric facility, walked to a 7-Eleven, and called the police department from a pay phone. He admitted to the nine-year-old rape and murder, which he knew about because he had once hung out with a gaggle of delinquents, drinking beer and smoking pot in those woods back in the early eighties. He spent many weeks in jail after this false confession and was front page news, scary Charles-Mansonish mug shot and all. My family came close to disintegrating. The mental pressure of being related to the stuff of headlines in our human-drama-driven, often exploitive, and regularly inaccurate media culture was hurricane-force, unrelenting. A very bad dream from which you cannot wake. Finally, once the cops understood the situation of his schizophrenia and ran some DNA tests, my brother was released to the custody of my parents and warned not to ever make a false confession again or he would be charged with impeding a police investigation. There was no article about his release in the local paper, at least not one I could find then or now, so for years people still thought he had killed the kid. My parents fearfully took my insane brother home because they couldn't find another place for him and he'd almost died as a homeless person a few years earlier, before the psychiatric ward from which he'd easily escaped. They never got over their guilt related to his homelessness, during which time he lost forty pounds and resorted to, just for instance, giving blow jobs to speed-freak truckers for donuts or coffee or pocket change.

I was in college in 1992, at the time of his false confession, hiding in my apartment, drinking 40-ouncers of the cheapest beer made and reading existential philosophy, the new journalists of the 1960s, and crime novels. A few months after his release, my brother—who had all but stopped sleeping and sometimes spoke in tongues—became convinced my parents' house had demons in it and that my father was somehow in control of them. He poured gas around the garage and through a central hallway and lit the house on fire. We had half a large can of gas, which is the only reason my family didn't die that night. But I already told you about this.

Jump ahead seven years. At the new trial in 1999,
Butler's version of events, put on with a straight
face and a professional demeanor by his white public
defender, shocked the dead kid's family and friends.
It went like this: Butler was drunk and high and he
and the dead kid—the thirteen-year-old Boy Scout and
active member in his church from a close and loving
family—had been meeting up regularly. The dead kid
was a prostitute, a super-secret sex fiend. Butler, as
usual, paid the kid for oral sex. Not satisfied, he told the
boy to take off his sock—just one. He wrapped the sock
around the boy's neck and anally penetrated him. All
consensual, according to the defense attorney. Butler
then passed out because he was so high. When he woke
up the kid was dead. Since my paranoid schizophrenic
brother had admitted to the fifteen-year-old murder
seven years earlier, he must have wandered by while
Butler was passed out and killed the kid. With the
available sock.

No kidding. The public defender *presented* this. The
dead kid's family hissed. Friends of the family booed
and shouted out. The judge called for order in the court.

My brother was then called as a defense witness. He
wore an orange jumpsuit and cuffs. The news ran one
of those coloring-book sketches of him on the stand
with the story since no cameras were in the courtroom.
I think the defense attorney and Butler thought he
was so whacked he'd admit to it again. Instead he sat
in the witness chair with eyes like something from a

novelty store, dropped the f-bomb several times, and cried out that he was innocent at a volume only a person living in at least two realities with very different sound perimeters could manage.

My brother went back to prison to serve the rest of his sentence for trying to kill my family. The jury came back with a verdict of guilty for Butler at near-record speed. The dead kid's family felt relief at the conviction and, I imagine, a soul-sickness, an existential earthquake, about what had been said about their long-dead son by a defense attorney and repeated in newspaper reports— reports everyone in their neighborhood and at their jobs and at their church undoubtedly read. Reports I've been rereading, all these years later.

The public defender was later asked by a reporter how he could do what he had just done—drag an innocent dead boy's reputation through the gutter like that with such a ridiculous story, such an absurd defense. He shrugged. He looked at the facts of a case before him, whatever case, and turned them into a story that had the best chance of getting his client exonerated. That was his job. He said what he needed to say to perform his job. He wouldn't apologize for that. But I think he *should* apologize. The one honorable mission is to look at the facts of a case and search for the heart of the matter, some truth. Increasingly that's not how our legal system, news media, and politics work. I know that's not a news flash, that it's barely worth mentioning. But it can drive a person a little crazy.

After the verdict, I holed up in my under-renovation farmhouse, feeling much as I had back in 1992 after the false confession, but now in my new and more comfy life away from criminals and the criminally insane. I mean, look at me: Advanced degrees, middle-class, forty-five-dollar haircut, trimmed reddish beard, cool new running shoes, sort of successful by Western, late-capitalist standards. But all this stuff—the crime, the mayhem, the violence, that slow, ongoing trickle of violence and stress throughout my life—man, it took a toll, it fucked me up. People live through much worse, of course they do, but whatever, because most of our existence is locked up right here in these house-of-mysteries skulls of ours, and *it fucked me up*.

I would later suffer a depression, a dark absence as physical as the flu, a grim floating distance from the life around me, that was very close to hospitalization, but I got over it, or got control of it, I guess, with heavy doses of intense mountain biking, diet and meditation, divorcing alcohol, readings in Zen Buddhism, hope in the language of liberal Christianity, my good fortune to have a stable marriage and professional life to hang onto, and writing, which I do not think of as a thing to do for money or a job, but rather as a way to try—*try*—to make sense of the regular absurdity and occasional shocking beauty of the human condition, which we can all ponder—if we like, if we are able—along our quick transit toward being forgotten.

But in 1999, confronted with all this again, I was, my mind was—the only accurate word I can think of—*convalescing* for a few weeks after the trial. I wasn't sure what to do, but I felt I needed to do *something*, and since I was a writer, mainly a student of the short story, with Anderson and Maupassant and Chekhov as my gods, but with some journalism background as well, and also a keen interest in the old sort of American-tragedy-reportage Crane and Dos Passos and Du Bois used to do, I thought I might try to write about this. I called the dead kid's family. I did know the boy back in the seventies. I'd played in his yard. I'd walked around in the woods where he was raped and strangled. I'd dreamed about him. I planned, first, to say how sorry I was—for his tragic death and for my brother's false confession, which caused them extra anguish in 1992 and then again in 1999, and for the bizarre second murder of their innocent child's reputation during that short circus of a trial. But the answering machine picked up. They were screening their calls to avoid people interested in telling stories about them and their dead son—to avoid, I realized, people like me.

Acknowledgments: Two sections of this book, in different form, previously appeared in *Texas Review* and were collected in the chapbook *Swallowing the Past*, published in a small printing by Texas Review Press in 2011. Two other sections, also in different form, first appeared in *Killing the Buddha* and the *Oxford American*.

Greg Bottoms is an essayist, story writer, and critic. He is the author of a memoir, *Angelhead*, two books of narrative essays about American self-taught religious artists, *The Colorful Apocalypse: Journeys in Outsider Art* and *Spiritual American Trash: Portraits from the Margins of Art and Faith*, and three genre-blurring collections of autobiographical short prose. He is a Professor of English at the University of Vermont, where he teaches creative writing.

W. David Powell is an artist and educator. This is the third book that he has illustrated for Greg Bottoms and Counterpoint. He lives in rural Vermont and is a Professor of Art at the State University of New York, College at Plattsburgh.